"Susan. No one is expecting you to be den mother of the month."

"I know so little about children, Griff."

"You know everything about loving people." He tilted her chin up. "I love you . . . for understanding. For being willing to have the kids with us. I want you to love them. But they're not perfect."

"Griff—"

"And there are many, many times when I have no desire whatsoever to think about my kids. As in, skip the children for now. Let's talk about the house. About a canoe trip up north. About how much I love you. About how damn much I want you at this minute."

His look of passion was so ardent that she could feel goose bumps rising on her flesh . . .

Jeanne Grant *is a native of Michigan, where she and her husband own cherry and peach orchards, and also grow strawberries. In addition to raising two children, she has worked as a teacher, counselor, and personnel manager. Jeanne began writing at age ten. She's an avid reader as well, and says, "I don't think anything will ever beat a good love story."*

Dear Reader:

One of the most exciting things about creating TO HAVE AND TO HOLD has been watching it emerge from the glimmer of an idea, into a firm concept, and finally into a line of books that is attracting an ever-increasing and loyal readership. TO HAVE AND TO HOLD is now nine months old, and that thrilling growth continues every month as we work with more and more talented writers, find brand new story ideas, and receive your thoughts and comments on the books.

More than ever, we are publishing books that offer all the elements you love in a romance—as well as the freshness and the variety you crave. When you finish a TO HAVE AND TO HOLD book, we trust you'll experience the special glow of satisfaction that comes from reading a really good romance with a brand new twist.

And if any of your friends still question whether married love can be as compelling, heartwarming, and just plain fun as courtship, we hope you'll share your latest TO HAVE AND TO HOLD romance with them and dispel their doubts once and for all!

Best wishes for a beautiful summer,

Ellen Edwards
TO HAVE AND TO HOLD
The Berkley Publishing Group
200 Madison Avenue
New York, N.Y. 10016

To Have and to Hold™

TROUBLE IN PARADISE

JEANNE GRANT

A™ SECOND CHANCE AT LOVE BOOK

Other books by ***Jeanne Grant***

Second Chance at Love
MAN FROM TENNESSEE #49
A DARING PROPOSITION #149
KISSES FROM HEAVEN #167
WINTERGREEN #184

To Have and to Hold
SUNBURST #18

TROUBLE IN PARADISE

First edition published June 1984

First printing

Printed in the United States of America

To Have and to Hold books are published by
The Berkley Publishing Group
200 Madison Avenue, New York, NY 10016

1

BALANCING A BULGING briefcase and a precariously filled white paper bag, Griff pushed open the front door. He set down both burdens long enough to shrug out of his camel's-hair sports jacket and hang it on a Victorian coat rack, the sole piece of furniture, as yet, in the hall. Silence and the smell of fresh paint greeted him, and he walked under the unique domed ceiling and past the round, leaded-glass windows in the dining room before entering the kitchen and again setting down the white bag—this time on a contemporary wood-topped counter.

Scraps of paper crunched under his feet, and like Hansel he followed the trail around the island counter in the huge kitchen until he came to a distinctly violet pair of corduroy pants and two slim bare feet.

The rest of Susan was hidden somewhere in the recesses of the deep bottom cupboard. Next to her toes lay a long roll of Contact paper, a pair of scissors, and a mound of discarded paper curlicues. Griff loosened his tie, leaned lazily against the counter, and surveyed the view.

Susan's fanny was a ten. There was no question about it. That particular slope from tapering waist to buttock to slim thigh should be licensed. Or taxed as a luxury item. His dark brown eyes narrowed, judiciously searching for a fault, and failing to find one. Griff had never really been all that hung up on fannies, but Susan's was frankly difficult not to appreciate. Clearing his throat to alert her to his presence, he said gently, "Do *not* bump your head, sweetheart."

He winced, hearing the immediate crack of bone against wood, followed by a muffled expletive not usually in his wife's vocabulary. The corduroys backed rather gingerly from the cupboard; then a pinkish top emerged. The garment was old and frayed and clung faithfully to Susan's high, firm breasts. Griff's eyes lingered, waiting. Next came a tousled cap of brown curls, followed by a slim hand shielding a new bump on the skull, and, finally, Susan's heart-shaped face turned up to his, her big gray eyes distinctly annoyed. But not at him.

"How late is it?" she asked guiltily. "And you're *here*, Griff. I thought you were going straight to the apartment after work."

"Those were the orders," he agreed. "You told me this morning, 'Griff, we've worked on the house every single night for nearly two weeks. Tonight we're going to eat at the apartment and just relax. Within a week, we'll be able to move in here for good anyway . . .'"

One eyebrow flicked up at his teasing. "The shop wasn't busy, and I thought I could sneak in a little more work before you got home. I don't want the house to look like a disaster area the first time the kids see it, and with Tiger coming this weekend . . ."

He nodded sagely. "The kids will really worry about whether the cupboards are lined. Considering we haven't got a stick of furniture in the place yet."

Susan uncoiled and drew herself up to a standing position. "You should have told me before we were married that you had this incurably sassy side," she told him gravely, brushing an imaginary piece of lint from his dark brown shirt. "Lining cupboards is very important. How do you think the dishes would feel on unlined cupboards?"

"I guess you'll have to tell me," Griff said, luxuriating in the sight of those big gray eyes with their short, dark lashes. Her cheeks were flushed, her soft lips bare of lipstick, and the cap of dark curls framed an incredibly creamy complexion. Not in any way strictly beautiful, Griff had told himself at their first meeting. Just . . . strictly beautiful.

"The dishes would be offended," Susan explained to him, like a nursery school teacher talking to a four-year-old. "They know this is our new home. They have to live in the dark as it is. Did you ever think of that? How would you like to be a dish? The least we can do is offer them fresh, new paper to sleep on."

For a pragmatic Norwegian, Griff seemed to thrive on her brand of nonsense. That private crooked smile of his came close enough so she could see the grainy lines of age and character on his square features before his lips touched down and settled on hers. His hands wasted no time; they never had. One pressed to the curve of her spine and the other splayed on her bottom, effectively pressing her full length to him. Like a fifteen-year-old boy, he was instantly aroused, the pressure of his male desire unmistakable against the fabric over her stomach. Just as instantly her breasts tightened, crushed against a loosened tie and broad chest. Anticipation danced happily through her veins, an anticipation Susan had never even envisioned in a man-woman relationship before she met Griff. Shy women could actually turn wanton, a revelation she was still discovering as she reluctantly pulled back from the peppermint taste of Griff's mouth.

"I promised you I'd have a roast all ready at the apartment when you came home," she said ruefully.

"You don't think for one minute I believed you?" He motioned to the white paper bag on the counter.

Her eyes widened as she peeked in. "*War sui gui?* Sweet and sour shrimp? And won ton soup, steamed dumplings . . . oh, Griff!"

Griff built a fire in the library, and they ate the Chinese food in front of it. After the meal, Griff sat on the floor cross-legged in front of the fire, Susan's head cradled in his lap on occasion. She kept popping up and down, roasting marshmallows on a twig. Images of Griff's children, Tom and Barbara and Tiger, kept popping into her head just as sporadically. Those few outings before the wedding had seemed to go well, but a foundation for any real relationship could hardly be started with an afternoon's romp in a swimming pool, or a couple of hours at a movie, or when that noisy clan got together for a dinner. The picture of those three pairs of eyes staring gravely at her during the marriage ceremony in the chambers of the justice of the peace still touched her heart. Yet suddenly Susan wondered if they hadn't been *too* grave, especially Barbara, with her perpetual aura of anxiety . . . *Darlings, I am not going to hurt you.* She was just so impatient to have them *here,* with her and Griff, a family unit loving and caring for each other.

For the next three weekends, the children would be coming one at a time—first Tiger, then Barbara, and finally Tom—so that Susan would have a chance to get to know each of them individually. After that, there would be visits on alternate weekends—or at least that was the stipulation in Griff and Sheila's divorce agreement. Actually, Sheila was only too happy to send the kids to Griff whenever she found their presence inconvenient, and Griff was delighted to have them as often as possible, though it still wasn't the same as having them full time, which both he and Susan wanted.

Absently, Susan popped another marshmallow into her mouth and settled back. "And we're not going to eat meals like this when your kids are here," she informed him, clearly expecting him to follow her train of thought.

He didn't seem to have any problem. "Our kids," he corrected, bending over to kiss her forehead.

"Our kids," she agreed, meaning it. She snuggled closer, sleepily half-closing her eyes as she surveyed the room and envisioned the rest of the house in her mind's eye. All her life, she'd been enthusiastic about contemporary architecture. Who would ever have guessed she would turn out to be a pushover for gingerbread?

The house was a Victorian white elephant, set in an

older section of St. Paul. Turrets and oddly shaped windows and bathtubs with feet; window seats and chandeliers; huge elms outside; a balcony *and* a fireplace in their bedroom . . . and space. Space for Griff's three offspring, whom she'd taken on with this new marriage of two weeks' duration.

He'd waved those kids at her like a red flag when he first met her. *Look at me. I'm just plain trouble.* He'd certainly told the truth, but his kids weren't the problem; as an only child, Susan cherished the thought of a large family. Her reservations had been about Griff himself, beginning with the fact that he was a divorced man. She'd successfully avoided the breed right up to the age of twenty-eight. Her mother had died when Susan was fourteen, but Susan had been old enough to remember and value that special relationship between two people who are willing to work at a marriage; today's easy-divorce society offended her. And Griff was not only divorced; he was also eleven years older than she, and his personality wasn't really her cup of tea. Then, too, his previous marriage made her nervous; with three children, there would inevitably be contact with the ex-wife . . .

The man had proved irresistible; that was the problem. Lord knew why. Susan hadn't been looking for love, nor did she appreciate dynamite. Physical men had always put her off. She liked bookworms like herself—men who took off at the speed of light when she said a polite no. Griff didn't acknowledge the existence of the word.

His hard thigh beneath the nape of her neck spoke for itself, with its tough sinew. Just above that hard thigh was a distinctly masculine appendage that never seemed to tire. Above that were muscular arms and a powerful chest. Yet there was a clever brain beneath all that brawn. Griff had inherited timberland north of Duluth, but he'd built up the two electronical components plants in St. Paul strictly on his own.

Susan's head tilted sleepily back, and she took a long look at him, just to make sure she hadn't forgotten any of the rest of her husband's features while he'd been at work. She hadn't. A square chin that no one argued with. Beautiful teeth—her own had cost her father a fortune in orthodontia. A straight nose and shrewd brown eyes that saw far too much. Thick, short, brushed-back hair—Norwegian blond, just like the hidden mat on his chest. And elsewhere. His face was still tanned from summer, weathered from thirty-nine years of living, and at times his eyes could darken with pain. Life's pain. Griff took so damned much in.

He could explode in temper or be gentle as a sleeping lion, but no one could guess, looking at him, how very hungry the man was for love. He was capable of incredible tenderness . . . Lazily, Susan stretched, her tired muscles protesting against the hardwood floor. Griff's thighs were a ton more giving.

Orange flames lapped up the chimney, snapping with enthusiasm. The fire cast elusive shadows on the empty bookcases, on the silver sconces over the fireplace, on the elaborate moldings of the ceiling. The room was starkly empty. There was no furniture—only a single bag of marshmallows and the remains of her favorite take-out dinner rested beside the hearth. The bay windows had yet to be curtained; the shelves were begging to be filled. The house was a beginning, just as their marriage was beginning, and Susan felt a crazy mixture of lush happiness and a strange restlessness of wanting to add substance to the dream, reality to the promise.

"Oriental rugs," she murmured. "We have to have Oriental rugs, Griff. It isn't the kind of house for wall-to-wall carpeting."

"Too hard to keep up."

"Hmmm."

He knew that velvet little "hmmm." An amused smile crossed his features as his finger touched her cheek. She lifted her face to his, baring her throat like a kitten requesting a stroking. The pads of his thumbs traced the soft lines of her cheekbones, then traveled down to the hollow in her throat. Her gray eyes closed.

Griff savored the curly head in his lap, the sweet

serenity that Susan so instinctively offered him. He had an urge to tuck her close and wrap her up. Since his divorce four years ago, no other woman had touched him the way Susan had. After the disintigration of his thirteen-year marriage, he hadn't wanted or expected another woman in his life, ever. Guilt over his children still preyed on him, and he felt an incredible weariness after the long-term marriage in which he had invested so much of himself had gone bad. He was brutally aware that he had more trials than gifts to offer in a relationship. He was not a man to invite any encounter when coming from weakness.

Susan had informed him he was a fool.

Griff knew better.

Yet he would have sacrificed a limb rather than lose Susan, and had felt that way from the instant he met her. The adjustments she would have to make because of his children—well, he would find a way to make that path smoother. There had been no honeymoon. Her choice. And the justice of the peace had been her choice as well. All she wanted was those first two weeks alone with him, she'd pointed out, and she *didn't* want some huge period of time before the children were invited into their lives. He'd heard her real message, that frills were not romance for her, that she derived less excitement from champagne and candlelight than she did than from simply being and loving and doing things together. *That,* for his lady, *was* romance . . .

Absently, he glanced out the darkened window. Ancient elms sprawled in the yard. Their leaves, dark green and turning brittle in the September chill, crackled black against the house by night. A restless wind was gathering force outside. "Hurry, hurry," the trees seemed to say as they hurled themselves against the gale. Winter was coming.

Not in this house. "Susan's castle" he'd named their rambling monster of a place; she'd brought her special brand of warmth to the fortress, a deep, true warmth he had not thought possible in his life. He stirred, stroking her hair one last time, aware of how tired his bride of two weeks was. Working all day in her store, then too many evenings on the new house, and God knew neither of them had spent much time sleeping once they did get to bed.

He was just as tired. A wee little empire, she teasingly called his multitude of business interests. That, her apartment and his, the new house . . . "Susan," he murmured.

Her eyes blinked open, a soft pewter gray. "We have to do Barbara's room first, Griff. Before she comes in two weeks. The boys might not care, but your daughter . . . We can completely skip the living room for now."

He propped her up and then smiled as he uncoiled his long legs and stood up. "For now, we can skip all of it. Let's get this cleaned up and head back to a nice warm bed at the apartment."

Susan yawned sleepily. "Powder blue or pale green for Barbara?" She sighed. "Tiger's so easy. A Minnesota Viking poster and bunk beds." She hesitated. "Maybe he won't want bunk beds . . ."

He bent over to kiss her forehead before gathering up their dinner debris. "Will you stop worrying about them? They've been camping out weekends at my place in sleeping bags for ages; none of them care about furniture."

"Hmm." She trailed him absently into the kitchen, snatching up the last Contact paper scraps from the floor to toss them in the trash.

"I heard that."

"Pardon?"

She glanced up to see the grin that was so uniquely Griff. One arched eyebrow and a slash of a smile. "Whenever I hear that little 'hmmm,' I know you're going to do whatever the hell you want to, regardless of World War Three."

Her smile was impish. "I never did believe in wars."

"You just set up mine fields in velvet." He shook his head ruefully and switched off the kitchen light. "We've got to put out the fire in the library—"

"Griff."

She'd had her mind on his three children for days. She was worried about whether or not they would accept her, desperately aware of how important they were to him, and uniquely conscious that their idyllic twosome couldn't last much longer. She'd known about his kids from the beginning, and she truly wanted to be a second mother to his brood. She might know nothing about child rearing, but she was not afraid of loving, and Griff himself had expanded that capacity for love within her.

Pinpricks of anxiety had gradually haunted more of her waking moments, yet at this instant, at this minute, Griff was standing in shadow, all tough sinew and moonlight-silver hair and dark, beautiful eyes. Hers alone. As male as danger, and sexual in a primitive way. He evoked vulnerability and he evoked desire, both still seeming strangers in Susan's cool, efficient, and well-ordered world. He'd encouraged her to break all her comfortable rules, yet she hesitated now, not sure how to ask for what she wanted. "We really won't have to go back and forth to the apartment much longer," she said hesitantly. "The kitchen's done, and the painting's finished . . ."

"We don't need to rush the move. All our clothes are still at the apartment; we can hardly commute from here to there to change for work."

"You're right," she agreed, turning away.

"We don't even have a bed in here yet."

"You're right," she repeated, and headed back to the library to take care of the fire. It had been an impulse, a silly, impractical impulse to stay here. To christen the house, just the two of them. In a week, the whole place would be livable—not fully furnished that quickly, but certainly inhabitable. They had a lifetime to spend in the house. There was no hurry.

She crouched down on the marble hearth. Their little fire was now only glowing coals; the large, shadowed room was hauntingly empty behind her. She adjusted the damper, set the screen in front of the fireplace, and stood up again, only vaguely aware that Griff hadn't followed her.

He was there, suddenly, in the shadows of the doorway, with a mound of sleeping bags in his arms and a cold draught of air following him that announced he had just been out to his car. He said nothing for a moment. The wind had whipped his blond hair, and with his square Nordic features and brawny build, she thought of him as Viking, an undeniably physical man with the inner strength of oak . . . and an incredible gentleness when it came to pleasing her.

"Our room, Susan?"

Something caught in her throat. "How dare you know what I'm thinking even before I do, Griff? I just can't imagine why I love you." She volunteered a kiss, took the pillows from the top of his bundle, and volunteered another kiss, then followed him through the dark, silent hall. Their staircase had a landing halfway up, with a long, low built-in window seat to match the long, low windows that stared out on their three acres. Normally, she would have been mentally hanging pictures and stuffing cushions for the window seat as she walked up the stairs. Not tonight.

Tonight her heart was full of Griff, and her mind was totally on him. On the intimate touch between them that she knew was coming. He was the kind of man who tried very hard to guess her every wish, who must have known hours before that she would want to stay here this night. He'd moved mountains to get her the house, just because she wanted it. And he'd moved her own private defensive mountains just to get her, making it very clear he'd be happy to treat her like spun glass if she wanted that. She didn't. She just wanted . . . Griff. His happiness was already irretrievably linked to her own.

Her thoughts strayed back to Griff's children, and the smallest of frowns etched her forehead. At the top of the stairs, one wing of the house was closed off by a set of double doors; there were four rooms where the original owners of the house had undoubtedly stuffed their offspring. Isolation tactics were not an element of Griff's concept of raising children, nor of hers. Tom was to have the first room in the main wing. It wasn't large, but Susan had already guessed that Griff and his seventeen-year-old son were fighting a few generation-gap battles; accordingly, she'd placed Tom far from his father's door. Tom of the winsome smile and lanky limbs and his father's pride—the boy just might appreciate a little privacy after coming in from a late date. The long conversation Susan and Tom had shared had been on the subject of energy and its effect on world politics; not the easiest topic to pursue at McDonald's, when the rest of the group were gregariously bickering about french-fry portions. Susan had not expected such a quick feeling of rapport with Griff's oldest child, but now she had high hopes they might develop it . . .

Across from Tom's room was Barbara's room. Or room-to-be. If anything could win over the girl with the snapping black eyes and fourteen-year-old world-weary precociousness, surely the room would help. That alcove was just made for a canopied bed; the perfect spot for a makeup table was just under the window. Barbara would need an extra bed for a girl friend to sleep in . . . or didn't girl friends spend the night anymore at Barbara's age? Surely, at fourteen, she wasn't already dating . . . ? Uncertainty flickered through Susan's mind, and her instincts told her to tread carefully with Griff's Barbara. The child hid her feelings very well beneath a torrent of teenage rhetoric, but the atmosphere between her and Susan wasn't friendly yet. How could it be? Susan would be taking her mother's place, a role she'd better step into very carefully . . .

"Susan!"

She rushed back to the hall, barely aware that she had wandered. Next to Barbara's room was a huge bathroom with a monstrous claw-footed tub and the original pull-down chain for the john. The light came from a crazy little skylight in the ceiling; sun-drenched by day, that corner was, in Susan's mind, already filled with lush ferns and other moisture-loving plants. She would find a small, fluffy rug that was colorful and soft, but not so big as to hide the patterned-tile floor.

The last room before theirs was to be Tiger's, and Susan unconsciously paused again. At ten going on ninety, that little imp had to be the easiest to win over. On first meeting, he'd dunked her in the pool. Not much on formalities, Tiger. There were certain priorities in life: What are you doing in my dad's life, strange lady, rated far below Can you swim? Throw a beach ball? They could cover one wall of his room with cork and fill it with color and brightness...

From the darkness, Griff's hand suddenly snatched hers, tugging her back out of Tiger's room. Most impatiently, she thought wryly. His arm whipped around her, hugging her close, and then nudged her unerringly in the direction of their room. Hunger had clearly replaced tiredness. It was most difficult to understand, when they'd just had dinner...

Their room was huge, with a marble fireplace in the center of the outside wall. Moonlight flooded in through four huge windows, and Susan felt a surge of emotion burst through her at the sight of it. The fireplace and gabled windows, the arched ceiling and molded walls...the room fairly shouted *family* to her. Births and deaths and wedding nights, laughter and tears and tenderness; she could almost feel the love of families that had known this room, a happiness of generations in their joys and heartaches.

Griff was laying out the sleeping bags by the hearth, and when he finished he walked over on stockinged feet to open the window a crack.

"It's pretty hard to take," she told him, not moving from the door.

"What is?"

"All this happiness."

His head whipped around. The strangest tightness filled

his chest as he looked at her. "Come over here," he said gruffly.

A glow seemed to suffuse her skin—a purely feminine glow. Her lashes fluttered as she glanced away from him; she could tempt a saint when she did that. Griff had never had one urge to be a saint. But before he could stride over to her, that lovely smile had been replaced by another worried frown.

"Griff, we really should do Tiger's room first. He's coming next weekend and . . ." She hesitated, then added firmly, "Listen. I know I keep talking and planning, but I don't want you to think I'm unrealistic. Of course we can't afford to do it all at once. But the kids' rooms—"

"Susan." In four long strides, Griff reached her and pulled first one of her arms and then the other around his neck. "You start the most ridiculous arguments," he murmured.

The kiss began in the center of her forehead, and gradually took in her eyes, her nose, the slanted, delicate bones of her cheeks. Griff cradled her head in his hands just so, his thumbs free to caress the firm line of her jaw. Damn, but the man made her feel like melted caramel.

"I wasn't arguing," Susan remembered vaguely, relieved to find she was still following the thread of conversation when his hands slipped down to the bottom of her sweater.

"You're worrying about the kids again. I want you to stop it." His fingers chased the pink sweater up and over her head. "You know I want them with us; you know I want to raise them because I love them, Susan, and because I want to give them what I feel they need . . . and more. But you, wife, are for the rest of my life, mate and lover. That's how I want to live with you; that's what I feel for you."

Griff's tenor voice could turn gravelly . . . at certain times. Susan flushed as his eyes gave out dark fires, running over her bare shoulders and firm breasts. She shivered suddenly, but he didn't smile; that kind of lightness suddenly didn't belong. He wanted her, in a possessive, purely male way; he needed to hold her, take her, protect her . . . reassure her. *Trust me,* his eyes demanded.

She did. Her fingers trailed up his chest to the first button on his shirt. Then the second. Longish blond hairs, silvery in the night shadows, sprang free under her fingertips. She could feel his heart beating strong and sure beneath her palm.

"And this business of expenses." Just slightly, his voice lost that certain seriousness, taking on a note of wry exasperation. "I've been trying to tell you for some time that I'm not a poor man, Susan. I lived in that small apartment only because I didn't have the time or the desire to take care of a bigger place—and I didn't have the kids with me. I'm not saying that alimony and child support won't limit the number of world cruises we can take every year, but we have no money problems. You can have your Oriental carpets, and you can buy the antiques you like, and you can keep your own money for your business, and you can do any room any damn way you want to. We've covered this before."

"Hmmm."

"Susan." Her eyes traveled up to his. "Don't *hmmm.* Not on this. I want you to have this house exactly the way you want it."

Too many married people argued about money. Susan was determined to avoid that pitfall. Having known Griff for three of the most exhilarating months she'd ever lived through, she was well aware that he was dreadfully overgenerous, particularly where she was concerned. By contrast, Susan hadn't bought a pair of shoes for the last nine years unless they were on sale. Obviously, compromise was occasionally going to be required in their relationship, as it was in any marriage.

And it definitely felt like her night to give in. She

finished unbuttoning his shirt, raised her eyes to his in the darkness, and whispered, "Just love me, Griff. Now."

Later, as she lay still in the darkness, Susan's eyes fluttered open. Moonlight filtering through the windows formed yellow-silver squares on the floor, but did not touch either of them in their sleeping-bag cocoon. Griff's leg was thrown over her thigh to keep her close to his warmth; his arm was still heavy on her side, and his hand still cupped her breast exactly as they'd been after they'd made love. The newlyweds lay in shadow, the room, and indeed the whole house, completely still. Susan listened to Griff's gentle breathing and closed her eyes again.

That first June night when she'd met him flooded her mind...

2

BARTHOLOMEW'S WAS ONE of St. Paul's best restaurants. When she walked in, Susan was wearing a mauve raincoat, a pale green dress, and her most brittle smile. It was ten minutes to eight on a hazy June night, a lazy sun just getting around to sinking below the horizon. And Susan was furious.

And nervous. It was all so ridiculous... Julie Anderson had a wine and cheese shop down the way from Susan's craft and book store. Julie's venture was new and not doing particularly well; Susan had offered moral support, and had somehow ended up brow beaten into accepting a blind date with Julie's older brother. Susan had last gone on a blind date when she was sixteen; the five-mile walk home had squelched any desire to repeat the experience. At twenty-eight, she couldn't have been less interested in wasting an evening, and she certainly should have had more sense than to get talked into having a drink with some strange man...

Beyond the entrance, she caught a glimpse of several rooms—three or four different dining areas and two bars. The entrance foyer held two couches, a fireplace, and wildlife prints, all rather subdued and peaceful. Unclenching her fists and removing them from the pockets of her raincoat, Susan settled in to wait, and was immediately approached by an efficient waitress. Wine coolers were on special.

Fine. Her throat was as dry as the Sahara.

The only reason she was here at all was that she figured Griff Anderson could hardly be a total nerd. He'd had the sense to call and cancel on the two previous occasions his sister had so cleverly set up. Which matched the two Susan had wiggled out of. He was obviously about as interested in blind dates as she was, but Gibraltar could be worn down more easily then the indomitable force that was Julie. So they'd make the gesture—one ten-minute drink together and the die-hard matchmaker would really have to let up, Susan figured. Certainly, as two mature people they could get out of having dinner together without undue awkwardness. So how bad could ten minutes be?

Setting down her empty wineglass, she glanced at her watch with a little frown. It was eight-fifteen. The room seemed increasingly warm, and she shrugged out of her raincoat. Beneath was the pale green dress she'd worn to work that day, a soft knit that clung lovingly to her slender figure. *Why* hadn't she remembered that Julie, the enthusiastic matchmaker, was a veteran field-player herself? "You think I wouldn't get married in a second if the right man came along?" Julie had insisted. "At least I've got the sense to keep looking. You two aren't even trying, and I just have the feeling that if you meet each other. . . ."

Lord, what hogwash.

"Would you like another drink?" The hostess hovered, smiling pleasantly.

"Well . . . all right."

Susan had already memorized every painting in the place, seen the ladies' room twice, and tested every chair in the foyer. She *knew* he'd said eight o'clock. The hostess brought a second tall wine cooler, and Susan settled back in the leather couch. She crossed her legs, then worried that it might look like a come-on and uncrossed them. Fine, he wasn't interested, but certainly the *least* he could do was be on time . . .

The hostess kept glancing at her. It was hardly the kind of place that encouraged lone women. Couples kept milling in and out. Susan gave her rapt attention to counting the bricks in the fireplace.

The wine had hit her like a submarine, but then she hadn't eaten any lunch. The problem was that her throat was so dry, and when the hostess offered her a third wine cooler, she nodded vaguely. The thing to do was leave, of course. It was past eight-thirty. She'd wait a few more minutes; she didn't want to pass up the opportunity to give Ideal Man—Julie's epithet, that—a piece of her mind. Leaving a woman waiting for better than half an hour . . . Susan had a few more creative epithets for Griff Anderson. Since they'd both agreed to this ridiculous meeting, she had a right to expect common courtesy . . .

At nine-ten, Susan set down her empty glass and was dizzily adjusting the shoulder strap of her purse as a tall blond man burst through the door. She caught a single glimpse, but was more immediately concerned with convincing her legs to hold her up straight so she could start moving. The derelict Viking was dressed in well-worn jeans, a tweed jacket, and bedraggled running shoes. He had a pair of shoulders that barely fit through the door, and a thatch of stark blond-white hair that should have been trimmed four weeks ago. She doubted the restaurant would seat him. His problem, not hers. She was going home.

She had raised her hand to push her way out through the heavy oak door when she felt a palm on her shoulder. Turning in surprise, she saw the Viking and caught a closer glimpse of his face. Deep-set dark eyes held a crazy mix of humor and stark sexual appraisal. A straight nose, thin lips—thin but sensuous—baring even white teeth in a crooked smile. Somehow the blend of features added up to passably handsome; her awareness of this fact annoyed Susan. That pair of lazy browns was busy communicating a very potent sexual come-on.

"Exch—excuse me," she said rigidly. She brushed his hand from her shoulder as she would flick away a gnat, trying to communicate politely to the stranger that she would prefer the touch of a bug to his touch. She attempted to take another step, but one long arm blocked the door.

"Just hold on. You were waiting for someone?"

"Jus' for you. To move," she slurred pleasantly. The flare of gun-metal gray in her eyes demanded that he do so. Promptly. Shy by nature, Susan seemed to have acquired instant assertiveness with the three wine coolers she had finished in the last hour. She was ready to take on all comers.

The challenge seemed to amuse the Viking; he delivered a smile from his six feet one down to her normally adequate five feet five. "You don't exactly seem to be in a receptive mood," he remarked.

She nodded. "You won't believe how my mood will improve once you get out of my way," she promised, and motioned again to his hand on her shoulder.

"If you'll calm down just a hair, I'd like to explain..."

So he required a sledgehammer. "Look. I am *tired.* I have been up since five; I have a headache; my plants need watering; and I have just wasted more than an hour on a man who's been a thorn in my side for nearly six months. Surely you must remember your mother telling you to show a little kindness to those less fortunate than you? Now's the time. Pick on someone your own size." She enunciated very clearly, in case he had a hearing problem.

The hand didn't move. She had a frustrated feeling that the man was struggling with laughter. She was struggling with dizziness. She tried again. "There's a brunette in the bar. All by herself. Amazon type. Very..." She explained the lady's figure by weaving an hourglass with her hands. "Really. You'd have to be out of your mind not to like her. Any man..."

The hand finally dropped, and husky laughter echoed through the foyer. Susan glanced around, embarrassed, and then hurriedly pushed open the oak door and started walking. Darkness had fallen, and the cool June night made her pull her raincoat closer around her. To her annoyance, the streetlamps were coming in double, and the parking lot had acquired a slant during the last hour. And a huge shadow loomed behind her from out of nowhere.

"The timing was bad. Tiger's on a Little League team. The game started at five and should have been over before seven, but it went into extra innings. I could still have gotten dressed and been here by eight o'clock but—"

She whirled, furious he had followed her—and then through a fogged brain realized that the Viking was actually the subdued, conservative businessman Julie had tried to pawn off on her. She took one more look, shuddered disbelievingly, and kept on walking.

"I could still have gotten here by eight," he repeated, "but the thing was, my son's team lost. The ball game."

"Look, Mr. Anderson," she started impatiently. She stopped beside her Mazda, opening her purse to find the keys.

"I took him for an ice-cream cone. It was the first game the team had lost," he said quietly. "Tiger struck out. What else could I do?"

She glanced up. The gun-metal gray of her eyes had softened to a rich, deep pewter. The bastard! If he'd handed out any *decent* line, she could have kept on freezing him out, but the image of a young boy coping with defeat, needing a soothing ice-cream cone . . . So his son came first with him. She respected that. Still, having started from a score of minus five hundred, he had only worked his way up to zero. "I'm sorry he lost," she said honestly, and bent her head over her pocketbook again. Kleenex, brush, lipstick.

"Can I help?"

She piled her brush, lipstick, and change purse into

his open palms. Three grocery lists, a dentist's receipt, the cameo that needed a new chain, the bracelet that snagged stockings, her checkbook.

"I *know* my keys are in here—"

"Have you had dinner?" He was struggling to keep his face straight. "Under the circumstances, I suppose that's a foolish question..."

"What's that supposed to mean?"

"Nothing," he said gravely. "I like an occasional drink before dinner myself."

"Well, I don't. Drink before dinner." She found the keys and unlocked the car door. A second later, she started shuffling her belongings from his overfilled hands back to her purse.

"Obviously."

"Pardon?"

"Obviously you don't usually drink before dinner," he said ironically. "By the way, you're not driving home," he added cheerfully.

"I shbeg your pardon." She frowned. That seemed to have come out wrong. "Your sister is a lovely person, Mr. Anderson—"

"Griff."

She waved her hands. First names were hardly worth quibbling over. "Now we've met each other. We don't have to fool around with this anymore. I really have to go home and water my plants." She slid into the driver's seat. She peered up at him, belatedly remembering her manners. "Really, it was very nishe to meet you. Very nishe. Julie told me what a wonderful man you are..."

"Pillar of the community, salt of the earth. All I lack is a nice little woman to ease the loneliness of a divorced man, someone who actually likes mothering children." He could quote his sister verbatim, she noticed. "And according to Julie, you were ideal. An attractive, quiet, shy little brunette, all alone. A craft and book shop. How...feminine. I had you pictured as a little paragon of virtue, a youngish maiden aunt. Move over, honey.

There's no way you're going to drive yourself home."

"Over my dead—"

His palm curled intimately under her bottom, shifting her over to the passenger side. Her legs promptly tangled in the stick shift, her green skirt fluttering back to reveal an expansive length of stockinged leg. "Now you just listen here—"

"How much? I'll reimburse you for the bar bill, since I'm responsible." He dipped down to grope for the dropped car key, rearranged her legs, covered her thigh again, and inserted the key in the ignition as he slammed the car door.

A moose wouldn't fit in a shoe box. He filled the car, but the engine that had been giving her such trouble purred like a kitten for him. *"Listen,"* she sputtered.

"Honey, it's all right," Griff assured her mildly. "I'll drive you home and call a cab to get back to my car. We can both tell Julie that we met and the mesh just wasn't there. I'll have my sister off my back for at least another month or two; you'll be happily tucked in your bed within an hour. No offense," he rushed in smoothly. "I don't mean to imply that you couldn't negotiate a straight line, but you belong in bed right now, curled up with a nice warm aspirin."

Susan settled back in a rather dizzy huff next to her door. *This* was the sedate, conservative, respectable captain of industry, the one so desperate for company, the one who never thought of anything but his children? His sister was under some terrible illusions. Those big dark eyes held more sexual experience than a spring day held sunshine, and as for his being hard up for female company...no. Not in this life. "You don't even know where I live," she protested.

"I think I can manage. Your address and phone number have repeatedly been given out to me for the last six months. In case I mislay any of my sister's notes, she calls regularly just to ensure—"

"I get the drift." She had been through Julie's water

torture herself. Griff shot her a look that reluctantly won a smile, and then a helpless little chuckle. Those big brown eyes just looked so long-suffering.

"My sister..." he began.

By the time they arrived at her apartment, Susan's alcoholic fog had settled into a pleasant sort of dizzy euphoria. He'd so nicely spelled out all the reasons why he very honestly wasn't looking for a relationship—in spite of his sister's best efforts. He was divorced. Divorced men were bad news. Susan wholeheartedly agreed. Having been married for thirteen years and divorced for four, he had no urge whatsoever to change his single state. In the meantime, he had three children and alternate-weekend visitation rights. Plus all the unscheduled visits he could get. The children had to come first in his life. Susan wholeheartedly agreed. At the time of the divorce, he went on, his kids were torn apart, and because he was a damn fool and confused at the time, he had let custody slip into Sheila's hands. The problem was that she wanted the money and not the children, and he was tearing himself up worrying about them. So as far as inviting anyone else into his life, knowing that somehow he was going to regain custody of his kids or die trying... it just wasn't the time for him to be looking for a wife, regardless of what his sister Julie thought about his bachelor state. Susan, once again, wholeheartedly agreed.

In fact, she agreed with everything he said. It confused her. Griff Anderson was telling her his life was a mess. At the same time, he created the impression of a man who knew exactly what he wanted, had figured out exactly how to get it, was big enough to admit his mistakes, and adored his children. As she snatched up her purse and opened her own car door, she was still trying to figure that out. She liked the man. She certainly didn't want him in her life, but she did like him. And despite his sending out all those *I am safe* messages, she had the terrible feeling as they walked up the sidewalk together that she would be making an irreversible mistake if she let him into her apartment.

He didn't give her much choice. For one thing, he had the keys...and was using them. For another, he had a crooked little smile that just dared her to object to letting a strange man into her apartment. Averting her eyes, Susan walked in as soon as he'd opened the door and flicked on a light. She hung up her coat, then waited patiently by the closet door for him to hand her his jacket, praying her double vision would recede shortly. He gave her the jacket, then walked past her and stood with his hands loosely on his hips as he surveyed the place.

The apartment was old, St. Paul style, on a street with huge, fat trees and thick ivy, close to the university. A pair of giant potted fig trees stood sentinel in the corners near two nubby beige chairs. The coffee table was Indian, intricate patterns of carved wood covered with glass. A twenty-pound aquarium occupied one corner, its light reflecting the darting moves of a half-dozen silver and fluorescent fish. Bookshelves, made from bricks and planks, surrounded the tank. Hanging plants dripped greenery onto a six-legged French desk that was two centuries old, her pride and joy. The couch was off-white, littered with a pink silk blouse and an open magazine. The effect, overall, was of a very personal and individual haven, Susan style.

Griff turned back to her, a glimmer of approval in his eyes. Her apartment, apparently, had passed some test...and so had she.

"The telephone's in the kitchen," she told him. "For the cab."

Obediently, he strode toward the kitchen, but she had a feeling he'd recognized her remark for the defensive ploy it was. She followed him, and gave a loud, expressive sigh when she saw him bending down to stare into the open refrigerator.

"You need food," he pointed out. "If you're going to drink on an empty stomach—"

"I *don't* drink on an empty stomach. I just don't drink. Normally. But I couldn't just play with my hands for more than an hour—"

"I know. I was late. And the very least I can do is fix you something to eat."

So virtuous. "It is *not* necessary."

"So . . ." He drew out a casserole of macaroni and cheese and looked vaguely around the kitchen. "We know you're not much on blind dates, that you can't handle alcohol, and that my sister has a better eye for a good-looking woman than I ever gave her credit for. You might as well tell me the rest of it."

He made the dinner. She watered the plants in between sips of strong black coffee and feeding the fish. By the time they sat down at the table, neither of them seemed to be wearing their shoes anymore. With the salad, he served aspirin for her headache.

He was a big believer in equal time, so over dinner she gave him all the reasons why she had been just as opposed as he was to being fixed up on a blind date. She had opened her book and craft shop five years before, with the help of a big dream, a very small inheritance from a distant uncle, a banker who actually seemed sympathetic, and a halfway decent collection of rare old books her father had contributed to the cause. *Undercapitalized* was the operative word. All of her time and energy had been channeled into getting the shop on its feet the last few years. Independence came to her naturally, as an only child, and perhaps also because her mother had died when she was young. She had only a father to harass her over her single state, which he did regularly from retirement in Arizona, a nice distance away. A nice distance away as far as harassment went—Griff mustn't misunderstand. She loved her father. In fact, ironically, her father was one of the main reasons why she had never thrown herself into the marriage market.

Her parents had been wonderfully happy—a tough act to follow, but Susan couldn't imagine setting her own sights any lower. And when her mom died, her dad had been wise enough to worry about filling his hours with things that counted to him. He didn't believe in seeking out relationships from sheer loneliness, nor in settling for less than the special love he'd had with his wife. Susan adhered to her father's own values. She wasn't panic-striken if she had to spend an occasional Saturday night alone. No, she wasn't brooding over someone from the past; there were no scars, no torches still carried; yes, she'd almost married once in college, but it hadn't worked out. Her father was getting a wee bit itchy for grandchildren. Well, occasionally she got a wee bit itchy for children herself, but the men in her age bracket seemed to equate maturity with bed immediately following dinner. The issue had become tiring. Maybe next year she'd figure out what was supposed to be such fun about waking up next to a stranger. For now, she passed.

When they'd covered all the reasons why they weren't interested in getting involved with anyone of the opposite sex in the immediate future, they did the dishes. The wine had diluted in Susan's system by that time, though a rather crazy, lighthearted feeling of elation remained. Griff kept her laughing; for some obscure reason, she seemed to keep him laughing, too. They were just strangers for an evening; no reason for defenses to be raised, no reason not to share a few blunt truths . . . but then Griff was the kind of man who evidently always played with his cards on the table. Being comfortable with his candor was a little difficult for Susan, who had always been more reserved. Proper. Griff already realized that.

Well, she was. Maybe not proper, but normally shy, modest, stiff with strangers. Where had all that old-fashioned stuff come from, she didn't know; her father had certainly been happily outgoing. It had always been a bit of a nuisance, carrying around those outdated character traits. With someone close to her, it was different, yet it had just never been easy for her to scale those defensive walls . . .

Griff had no problem. How or why it happened

. . . She was doing something simple: hanging up the dish towel. His hand brushed the small of her back. And then lingered.

She turned to him with a smile all ready to be captured. He captured it. That first taste of a shared kiss seemed to surprise them both, because suddenly there was no more laughter. His arms cradled her close as if he'd discovered something precious. A blend of rough, tender kisses aroused a sweet, low love song in Susan that she'd never heard before. He had so damned much love in him, all pent up. She could feel it. Touch it. It was not the desire to take, but the desire to share, the need to share, the need to touch another human being . . .

Susan knew better than to sleep with a man she barely knew. It had never happened; it never would happen.

But then she didn't sleep with him; they didn't *sleep* at all. They made love, over and over, defining that word in all its myriad facets. Tenderness, sharing, selflessness, warmth, passion . . . touching souls. For the first time in her life, Susan understood why she had built up so many defensive walls over the years. Anything casual would have taken away from what she offered this man now. What she wanted to offer him, what he asked for, what he claimed, was the freedom to share the depth of emotion she had kept inside herself. She was like a well just waiting to be tapped, straining to be free . . .

They were married at the end of August, almost three months later. The small, simple ceremony had seemed so right to her, only the people who really mattered to both of them sharing that very private commitment. Her father had flown up ahead of time to spend the week, wanting to get to know Griff. The two men had known each other only an hour when her father had cornered her. "So you finally found him, Susie." There had been a sweet blur of tears in his eyes at the ceremony; Julie had been wearing an I-told-you-so smile, her hands filled with rice . . .

Susan smiled sleepily and curled an arm around Griff

in sleep. The house was so quiet; the air so still and fresh; the last of summer's sweetness drifting through the partly open window.

She was worried to death that his kids wouldn't like her. She was just as concerned that Griff wouldn't get the custody he so desperately wanted. She was well aware that he was trying a bit too hard to pretend he never lost his temper, that he enjoyed cooking, and that he didn't care if she had to work an occasional evening in the shop. She was just as aware that she'd never really anticipated being involved with the kind of no-hold-barred physical and emotional man that Griff was, and she was fighting a few feelings of inadequacy, of doubt that she was up to providing the depth of love he needed so much.

She closed her eyes. They'd work it through. She had never been so sure of anything in her life. A love this strong, this rich...Come on, world, we're ready, her heart sang, and the song became part of her dreams.

3

"No. Try it like this, Mrs. Riffler." Susan glanced wildly at the clock, then pasted on a calm, reassuring smile for her elderly customer. "The tension of the yarn is important. Just try it once more."

"I swear it never seems to work for me like it does for you. Maybe if you'd do this little part for me..."

Susan ran a distracted hand through her thick, dark hair, but her smile never faltered. "Of course."

It was past noon, and Griff was expecting her. He'd gone to fetch Tiger from his ex-wife for the weekend, and the three of them had a thousand things planned. She'd only stopped by the store to do an hour of bookkeeping—and found her assistant, Lanna, trying to keep the shop open even though she was running a temperature of 101 degrees. Susan sent Lanna home. It didn't matter; the shop always closed at noon on Saturdays... except that Mrs. Riffler had never appreciated the significance of closing time.

Sunlight filtered in on the unicorn display in the front window. Susan had displayed images of the mythical creature in crewel, in wood, and in pastels, all on easels designed to catch the customer's eye. Beneath the three frames were whimsically jacketed books of myths and monster legends and fairy tales.

Susan had always had a strong love of books; she'd

collected more books than dolls as a child and had worked in bookstores from the age of sixteen. Her father's hobby was trading and swapping old editions which he'd passed on to her for her shop. During her last year in college, an uncle on her mother's side had died and left her an unexpected inheritance. It was enough for a down payment on a corner building that contained a small apartment above a store, very close to the university. Up to that point, her dream of owning a bookstore had always been wishful thinking.

Reality was far different from the dream. Who would have thought one small bookshop could have had such an enormous overhead? Thank God for the bank's friendly loan officer. Finally, the store was stocked, the image of her youthful dreams; but then she made a series of dreadful mistakes. Getting people to come into the store was no problem, but old editions brought browsers, not buyers. The college kids loved to haunt her back aisles, where they thumbed through her expensive reference materials until the pages were dog-eared. And that unique section of children's literature she was so proud of brought in the little ones, all right, but books with crayon marks just didn't sell. Desperate by then, Susan had branched out into crafts—needlepoint and crewel, crocheting and candlewick. She'd started giving craft classes herself. Susan would have sold kisses for a dollar apiece at that point, but actually what was required was much more careful buying of items that would bring in ready cash and encourage paying customers. Reference materials were now stocked behind the counter; she'd started a used and new children's section... there had certainly been some changes made.

A great deal of scrambling had been required over the last five years, but Susan was now close to paying the last debt on that corner lot, and she rented out the apartment above the shop to Lanna—a recent college graduate and a book fanatic like herself who had proved invaluable both as friend and worker. Every inch of the struggle had been satisfying, even the occasional prolonged visits by lonely widows like Mrs. Riffler. The older woman beamed at her, finally stuffing her half-done afghan into her huge bag. "I just knew you wouldn't mind if I came down to have you show me the stitch again. You know, I used to go to that other craft shop on Fifth Street, but they never had the time..."

Susan locked up and whipped down the window shades.

"And I hear you just got married? I think it was Mrs. Wilding who told me. Just the thing, just the thing. I never could figure out, with you being so sweet and pretty..."

God in heaven. Susan bit the inside of her lip, not an easy thing to do when one was smiling, and resisted the urge to lift one foot and then the other impatiently. At last Mrs. Riffler ambled off in the opposite direction. Susan walked sedately to the corner, turned out of sight of the building, and took off at a dead run for her car.

A little breeze was stirring on the tree-lined street, but the sun was beating down as if it were mid-July. This year autumn would be late; a long, hot summer was lingering in the warm days. Susan hustled into the driver's seat of her Mazda and burrowed for the car keys in her purse at the same time as she hurriedly tried to roll down the windows. The little car was stifling.

Stabbing the key in the ignition, she caught a glimpse of herself in the rearview mirror and snatched up her purse again. She looked terrible. There were circles under her eyes; her hair needed a styling... They'd been working so hard on the house, and Griff had worked even harder than she had. It was at the fun point, though, really. The plaster dust and the painting debris were gone; now the name of the game was curtains and paintings and furnishings... at least for her. Griff was building storage cabinets in the basement; insulating; he'd insisted on a new furnace...

She brightened her cheeks with blusher and fluffed up her curls with a hairbrush. All that adrenaline pumping in her veins urged speed, yet still she took another second for a quick spray of perfume and a last glance in the mirror. Griff *would* notice what she looked like. He would also be extremely difficult to live with if she seemed the least bit tired. Rather like the domineering male counterpart of a mother hen.

The car engine seemed to feel it had done enough running all week. Susan generously gave it four more opportunities to change its mind. It ran for Griff, dammit. What *was* it he'd told her to do? Something about punching the thing or keeping her foot off the accelerator if it flooded. And when all else failed, swear. All right, then... Subjected to Griff's colorful language, the engine promptly zoomed, and shortly after that Susan was zigzagging through traffic. Actually, she thought wryly, her Mazda was just smart enough to know Griff had threatened to buy her a new car.

Twenty minutes later, she jammed on the brakes in the driveway, only to discover Griff's car wasn't there. Impossible. The drive to Sheila's and back couldn't have taken an hour, and two hours had passed. Susan snatched up her purse, opened the car door, and decided to just breathe for a minute and a half. Truthfully, she was grateful for these few moments. This was the first occasion when they would really have Tiger for any period of time since the wedding. Yes, those prenuptial outings had always gone well, but she hadn't been Griff's wife—or his children's stepmother—then. Tiger—officially Charles Griff Roth Anderson—could well come up with a suddenly different reaction to her, once he realized she was here to stay.

Her toes hadn't connected with the cement driveway before Griff's Mercedes station wagon appeared beside her. She didn't even need to see Griff's face to know that something was wrong. He was not the kind of driver who lurched to a stop, nor did she miss the crisp thud of a slammed door, though Tiger bursting out of the car took all of her immediate attention.

"Hi, sweetie," she said affectionately, and offered open arms.

Tiger swung into them. She wasn't kidding herself that the hug meant anything yet—Tiger hugged stray dogs, too—but at least there was no hesitation in his warm, wriggling body as he grinned up at her. "Looks like a neat place. Any secret passages?"

She had been waiting for that one. "A dumb dumbwaiter."

"A dumb dumbwaiter?" Tiger echoed, all instant fascination.

Susan chuckled. "I'll show you, kid. And I can hardly wait till you see your room."

He took off for the door, and Susan, still smiling, headed for Griff's hug. He was ready for her, but his arms squeezed her so tightly that she glanced up. Those dark brown orbs were full of storm; not to mention the tension she could feel in his heartbeat, in the arms still wrapped around her shoulders. When she left that morning, he'd been in a wonderful mood. "What's wrong?" she whispered.

"Nothing," he said tersely.

She almost shivered. When his emotions were all leashed up, Griff could be a dauntingly formidable man.

"The door's locked," Tiger called back to them, clearly disappointed.

"I've got the key." Susan glanced once more at Griff, then turned helplessly to his son.

Tiger was more than ready to claim all her attention. He had to explore the dumb-as-in-nonfunctional dumbwaiter immediately; then he raced through each room, opened drawers and abandoned them, tested lights . . . To Susan's eyes, he was a beautiful child, all blond hair and big dark eyes like Griff. He was simply his father in miniature, carefree, mischievous form; how could anyone help loving him? His jeans were too short for him, and his old sweatshirt had the number twelve on it . . . as well as a hole in the shoulder. Obviously favorite old clothes, she thought affectionately as she raced up the stairs after him. In another year, he would doubtless be all gangling legs and arms.

"This is it? *My* room? The one I get all to myself?"

Laughing, Susan stood behind him. "Oh, Tiger, I could hardly wait for you to get here. We thought about doing up this room first thing, and then decided we'd wait for you. This afternoon, we want you to go with us and pick out exactly what you'd like. I thought maybe you'd prefer bunk beds and blue carpeting; you told me one time you liked blue. I don't mean we're going to drag you shopping all afternoon, just that we want you to show us the kind of thing you like..."

Griff stepped into the room behind them. Tiger glanced back at his father uncertainly, and Susan again felt the strange tension emanating from her husband. Her smile never faltering, she leaned back against Griff and dragged his arm around her waist. "No bed, Tiger. But we've got a sleeping bag for this time, or you can sleep on the couch downstairs, and by the time you come for the next weekend—"

"When he comes next time, we'll *have* our kind of weekend," Griff interjected flatly.

"Pardon?" Whatever was he talking about?

Tiger looked at his dad again and shrugged nervously. "Mom kind of gave me this list, Susan." He dug a wrinkled piece of paper from his jeans pocket. "Like I don't know. Mom said this is what we were supposed to do."

She unfolded the piece of paper: four pairs of pants, three dress shirts, four play shirts, tennis shoes, socks, a winter coat, dress shoes...It didn't take Einstein to figure out why Sheila had deliberately decked out Tiger in too-short jeans and a holey T-shirt. So much for favorite old clothes. And since Griff paid out more in child support in a month than Susan earned in a year at her store, she now knew exactly why Griff was barely controlling his temper.

Disappointment flooded through her for the day planned with Tiger that was not to be. Susan only had to glance once at the child to know she would follow through with Sheila's plan and not with their own. Griff was clearly furious, and just as clearly anticipating ignoring his ex-wife's wishes . . . but Susan was the one on the tightrope. Not for a lapful of diamonds would she cause friction between Tiger and his mother, nor would she confuse her role with Sheila's. "Perhaps if we can get through the list, we could still—"

"Bugs," Griff snapped succinctly.

"Bugs?" Susan echoed vaguely. Not really her favorite topic of conversation. And certainly a nonsequitus. Whatever did bugs have to do with anything?

"For school," Tiger volunteered. "I've got ten already. But if I can get another fifteen by Monday, I can put them in this science exhibit at school. Only I won't have time to find them, because Aunt Lisa's birthday party is tomorrow, and Mom's picking me up tonight, because she said she wouldn't have time to come after me tomorrow."

"I see." She saw. Sheila was violently opposed to Tiger spending any time with Susan and Griff.

She had agreed oh-so-sweetly to the consecutive weekends, no doubt all the while laying her plans for sabotage. It had been one thing for Sheila to dump the kids on Griff—an unmarried Griff—at her convenience. But Griff-and-Susan, who just might strike a family court judge as more suitable guardians for the children than Sheila, was another matter.

"You can't even spend the night then, Tiger?" She had planned to make pancakes piled three high for breakfast, then maybe a romp in the park and an early Sunday afternoon movie. For that matter, Griff had been sure that Tiger would enjoy puttering around with the two of them in the house . . .

"I'm not supposed to, Susan," Tiger said simply. Anxiety clouded his eyes as he waited uncertainly for her reaction, evidently having already gotten his dad's.

Sheila's manipulations weren't his fault. Susan reached out to rumple Tiger's hair. "Well, we'd better get going, kiddo. We've got a lot to do this afternoon," she reassured him. Like shopping. And bug collecting. What on earth were they going to collect bugs in? They were still setting up the house and living out of boxes.

"I don't think so," Griff said ominously. "His mother is well aware that he has plenty of clothes. Less than two months ago—"

She felt Tiger tense up beneath her hand on his shoulder.

"So he goes through a lot of clothes," Susan said swiftly.

"Tiger, you're not going to tell me you outgrew everything—"

The boy looked lost. "I've got lots of clothes," he agreed. "And I told Mom I didn't even want a new pair of tennis shoes. But she said I had to have new stuff. Something about you having the money for the new house and everything."

Susan stepped in front of her husband in an instinctive desire to stave off a tornado. "I got pretty attached to a pair of tennis shoes myself as a kid," she said lightly, "but you'll have to help me with the rest of the clothes, Tiger. I don't know much about boys' sizes. If you'll hustle downstairs, we'll be there in two seconds."

Or three. As Tiger was clattering down the stairs two at a time, Susan looked at Griff. He'd turned stranger, her volatile but always considerate lover. His mouth was a slash of white, his eyes were ice cold, and he gave off tension like an aura. "That bitch," he hissed.

The blood turned cold in her veins, racing up to her head. Griff in a temper, even though she knew it wasn't directed at her...

When Griff saw her color change, he immediately backed off, shocked at that tiny flicker of fear in Susan's eyes, more shocked that he could conceivably have evoked it. "Come here," he suggested quietly.

She did, and he folded her close to his still pounding heart. Dammit, he was mad in her behalf. Sure, he *could* force the issue of his son staying for the weekend. And he damn well knew his son didn't need new clothes. But the real fury came at the thought of Sheila's deliberately causing a problem for Susan. He knew exactly how much the very vulnerable, very feminine woman in his arms had been looking forward to planning Tiger's room with the boy, that it was a chance for the two of them to get to know each other . . . and that Susan was miserable at the thought of making any waves. He could put his foot down, all right, but Susan would suffer for it.

"Darling . . ."

Susan pulled free, looking up at him. "It doesn't matter," she insisted.

"It *does* matter."

She shook her head, making for the door. "Griff, the point is that we have time with him. What we do during that time isn't all that important." She hesitated and tried out a tentative smile. "Besides, I'll buy a few things in the next size up, so this can't happen again. And he can keep a few clothes here. Then he won't have to pack when he comes for a weekend. It'll be fine. Really."

It wasn't exactly fine. After fifteen minutes, Tiger had as much interest in shopping as in a dentist's drill. Also, he liked only red shirts with alligators on them. The stores seemed to stock blue and brown shirts—and no alligators in Tiger's size. His feet were hard to fit, and his conversation was blandly peppered with "Mom said . . ." Griff had come along to help, but Susan had banished him to the hardware section when she saw he was becoming impatient with Tiger, particularly on her account.

As soon as his father was out of sight, Tiger delivered a long dissertation about hamsters—when he wasn't vaulting up and down escalators to the peril of fellow shoppers. Santa Claus couldn't have talked him into accepting a new pair of tennis shoes; his old ones were like friends.

Griff caught up with them again. All discussions of small animals ceased. They sedately took the elevator, and Griff carried the scorned sneakers.

Tiger and Griff had worked themselves into a good humor by the time they got home; only Susan was distinctly wilted. She would have bargained with the devil for a cup of coffee at that point, but instead there were the bugs to worry about. Sheila was picking Tiger up at six. "Which leaves us two hours to find fifteen bugs. As in collect, catch, murder, pin, and label?" She wanted to make sure she understood the assignment properly.

Griff gave her a look.

"Dispose of," she amended, seeing that he seemed to find something strange in her use of the word *murder*. Hurriedly, she found a stack of empty margarine containers and started handing them out. "You men do the collecting, and I'll arrange the bugs on the display board."

"Susan, you don't have to be involved in this," Griff said firmly.

Well . . . she did, actually. Tiger was clearly enthralled with entering his science fair, and Sheila had just as clearly abdicated her responsibility in this area. Susan desperately wanted to find her own private little niche to share with Tiger. She knew nothing about ten-year-old boys. In the back of her mind, she'd figured on doses of love and gin rummy, and doses of love and his room, and doses of love and maybe checkers—but not bugs. Or having to force one disgusted little boy through two tedious hours of shopping. At least he was interested in the bugs—she'd have to take her chance where she found it.

She was heating a pot of water for coffee when the first margarine container arrived, via one small filthy hand. "Can you believe it? A stinkbug!" Tiger caroled enthusiastically.

"Aaah."

How nice. She added two spoonfuls of instant coffee to her cup, and watched warily as the plastic container suddenly jumped a half-inch off the counter. Clearly, the thing was alive. And she was the one who had volunteered to kill and pin it. Perhaps the coffee would fortify her.

With her chin cupped in her hands, Susan watched an incredibly rapid progression of insects arrive. Who would have thought that collecting them would be so easy? The backyard looked spotless. Clean, well kept. Yet in came long-horned beetles, short-horned beetles, crickets, grasshoppers, a lacewing, a stone fly, and Tiger's favorite, an assassin fly...

Assassin. Her job. By the time Susan had finished her coffee, she'd unearthed a square of plywood from the basement and meticulously printed out fifteen labels, all neatly attached to the board now. The opposite counter was a circus act of jumping margarine tubs. She was feeling distinctly sick to her stomach.

The back door flew open yet again, this time propelled by a much larger hand than Tiger's. Susan lurched instantly to her feet. "How's it going?" she asked cheerfully.

Griff watched her busily transferring all the bug containers to the kitchen table. Such busy-busy movements for his normally graceful Susan...His eyes swept over her supple lines in the soft mauve shirtwaist. Those butter-soft eyes were fluttering away from him, hands nervously rearranging her hair and her collar—in between trips back and forth to collect the bug containers.

He cleared his throat, setting yet another one on the table. "A bumblebee. God knows what one was doing in the yard this late in the season."

"We needed a bee," she said gravely. "I can't tell you how worried I was that we weren't going to have a bee."

The chuckle came from deep in his throat, just before his hands snatched her up and swung her close to him. She smelled delicious. Susan always smelled delicious. At the moment, a wee bit like coffee and felt-marker ink, but beneath that he could easily detect the faint scent of the perfume she wore, and the undeniable Susan-fragrance of soft skin beneath that. His lips snuggled in at the side of her neck, just for one small bite—

Susan nipped back, wound her arms around his waist and looked up at him. "I want to talk to you."

"So talk." Communication was terribly important in a marriage. His hands swept down the supple slope of her back to her waist, communicating terribly important things. Delicate color rose in her cheeks, delighting him. She was getting all the right messages. Tiger could do his own damn bug collecting.

"About hamsters."

He drew back, eyebrows arched. "Hamsters?"

"Tiger wants one so badly, and Sheila doesn't want to be bothered."

"One of the few things in life I agree with my ex-wife on."

"Hmmm." Her fingers chased up a wandering trail until both her arms were loosely hooked around his neck. He smelled as fresh as the autumn breeze outside, all woodsy and male. "It would be something he could have here. Special for him. That his mother couldn't possibly resent. And if it's so important to him..."

"Darling." He pressed his forehead to hers. "Hamsters smell like the pits, are a great deal of work and mess with little return—and my son, hard though this may be for you to believe, will survive without one. Now a dog—"

"Would be nice. But he wants a hamster."

"Have you ever had a hamster?"

She shook her head. "Cats and fish."

"We'll get a cat, then. You've already got the fish."

He extricated himself from her reluctantly, seeing Tiger approaching from the window over the sink. His son inevitably came through a door as if he lived in constant fear that the knob wouldn't work. The effort was usually a crash-through, as noisy and clumsy as possible. Tiger's brilliant smile inevitably made up for that.

"Can you believe it? I've got three more. How many we got now, Susan?"

Susan viewed the table impassively. "Thirteen."

"Well, come on, Dad, we're nearly done."

Griff's sigh reverberated through the kitchen as he turned and followed his son. "Susan?"

She looked up from dolefully regarding the collection. Her smile, by contrast, was remarkably brilliant. "I was just about to start killing them," she said happily.

"Susan—"

"You just go right ahead."

"A drop of alcohol. It's a quick, painless death," Griff said wryly. "And if it's really bothering you—"

"Of course it isn't!" she said indignantly. What did he think she was, some kind of sissy?

"And Susan, no hamsters."

"Hmmm."

They didn't seem to have any rubbing alcohol. Vaguely, Susan remembered throwing out half a bottle when she'd packed up the things from her apartment, but no amount of poking through the medicine cabinets revealed one now. Glancing out the window, she saw Griff in the far corner of the yard, laughing at something Tiger said, and guiltily pulled his bottle of Chivas Regal off the top shelf of the kitchen cupboard.

It *was* alcohol, she defended herself. She sat down at the kitchen table, rearranged her skirt, smiled for her own benefit, and, with the first drop of scotch, dosed a simple housefly. Having willingly swatted thousands of them in her lifetime, she decided that the fly would be the easiest to deal with. After a minute, she carefully peeled the lid open just a little, to find the fly still groggily winging around. Her stomach turned over. She dosed the insect with three more drops, and opened a second container.

A dreadful acrid smell assailed her. The stinkbug. She'd thought Tiger was joking. She jammed that lid on again and checked out the grasshopper, who looked distinctly innocent, harmless, and deserving of life.

She jammed that lid on, too, and checked the fly again. Murmuring a short eulogy, she gingerly lifted the tiny corpse with tweezers, transferred it to the mounting board, jabbed it with a pin, and swallowed hard against her revulsion. This was ridiculous. They were only bugs, dammit. She was no shrinking violet, and had certainly swatted her share of mosquitoes every summer.

All too soon, Tiger would probably be bringing home

snakes. This was nothing. So where was her sense of humor?

But Susan knew what was really bothering her, and it wasn't the bugs. A few painful realities were stabbing at her consciousness. Feelings of inadequacy haunted her. Whatever had made her think she was equipped to deal with a ten-year-old boy who had dropped into her life out of the blue? She knew nothing of his interests, so why had she blithely assumed she could easily occupy a special little niche in his life? Yet that's what she wanted, not to be a mother to him, but to be someone who was special in another way, someone who really cared, someone he could grow to count on...

She already loved Tiger, but this was their first one-to-one encounter; and she really *didn't* understand the monumental importance of red shirts with alligators. Usually so composed, she had quickly lost patience when Tiger was vaulting up and down the escalators in the stores, and as for the squirmy, germ-ridden bugs in her spotless kitchen...

We *do* tend to overreact on occasion, Susan told herself wryly, and picked up the bottle of Chivas. At least the bugs were going out in style.

4

" 'A LITTLE WATER clears us of this deed,' " Susan murmured to herself several hours later as she slid deeper into the warm bath intended to obliterate all trace and memory of her afternoon of bug killing. The blend of water and darkness invoked a lush, lazy sensuality in her. Submerged in clear, scented water to her throat, she leaned her head back against the porcelain tub and regarded the bathroom through half-closed eyes.

A bathroom was a rather eccentric place to put a twenty-gallon aquarium. Weeks ago, when the house was redolent of plaster dust and the pungent scent of fresh paint, it had seemed the safest choice. Now, Susan had discovered that the aches and worries produced by even the most grueling day dissolved after a few minutes of a hot bath in darkness, with only the dim fluorescent light of the aquarium and the soothing sound of the bubbler intruding on her consciousness. The pale blue iridescence illuminated the room with soothing, sensual tranquillity, and the silver fish weaving in and around their watery greenery had a subtle, hypnotic effect.

The bathroom had obviously been a small bedroom once. It had been converted in the way of Victorian houses at the turn of the century, like a lavish afterthought. The room was too big, but the skylight was wonderful; in daylight the sun's rays streamed lavishly down on the tropical plants in the corner. Now she could see stars through the window to the night. The gleam of brass fixtures, the velvety blue throw rug she and Griff had found, the corner of lush greenery, the blue glow from the acquarium, and the hush of night around her . . . Half-smiling, Susan closed her eyes.

When she opened them again, Griff was standing over her. There was a jackhammer pulse in his throat as he watched her. She had no idea how long he'd been there. A pale towel was draped around his hips, and his silver-blond hair had a slick sheen; she knew he'd showered some minutes before. He said nothing for a moment. Only played a thousand and one intricate little games with those dark sensual eyes of his resting on hers in the semidarkness.

He could see her skin, all white satin beneath the water in the aquarium's glow, breast and stomach and thigh. By contrast, he stood in the half-dark, just the gleam of that leonine head and the expressive eyes glinting. His broad shoulders were all in shadows . . . and distinctly bare.

"I was afraid you'd fallen asleep," he said quietly.

She shook her head, instinctively leaning forward and drawing up her knees. He chuckled, almost an imperceptible sound, as if he had read the wild fantasy in her head—that he was a pirate, that she was defenseless. "What did you think I was going to do?" he whispered.

"Nothing." She leaned her chin on her knee, her eyes never leaving his. "It's not possible, Griff."

"What isn't?"

"Stop thinking it. We'd both drown."

"What on earth makes you think you know what I'm thinking?"

"I *know*. Behave yourself."

The towel dropped just that promptly. She should have known better than to issue a challenge. Or anything he could have taken as a challenge. He stepped into the huge, claw-footed tub with her, sat down, and slid his legs under hers, pulling her close. Neither of them was comfortable. Griff's brows furrowed together, and Susan smiled. He rearranged her legs until they were stretched out behind him and she was straddling his hips; then the furrow left his forehead, and she was no longer smiling. Her skin, like damp silk, took on an erotic flush at the intimate contact. Water now lapped at her nipples instead of her throat; her breasts were displayed like white satin orbs in the water, less than inches from the damply curling hair on his chest. Her bottom was possessively anchored between his thighs, and she couldn't possibly ignore the portion of his lower body that was like steel beneath the water. Silk steel. He fooled no one by picking up the soap. They were both already clean ten times over.

"Griff, you're crazy," she whispered helplessly. "The tub isn't big enough..."

He drew a circle around her breast with the edge of the soap. Then the other breast. He rinsed both off with his hands. "You are," he said thickly, "a uniquely beautiful woman."

"Griff..."

Not so very long ago, she'd been very shy where intimacy was concerned. But shyness was useless around Griff. He set the soap aside and leaned back for a moment, deliberately not touching her. Her flesh became almost painfully sensitive as she felt his eyes possessively sweep over breast and thigh and velvet triangle, then meet her eyes with a lion's hunger. And a man's need.

Shyness left her, and a surge of love took its place. The shadowy glow from the aquarium illuminated the brawn of his damp shoulders and hair-roughened chest, the power and almost savage intentness in his features. Ripples of erotic awareness hurried her heartbeat, yet that wasn't all that made up that sweet rush of love.

She'd loved watching him with his son. He'd never asked Tiger how he'd been doing, but in the course of the afternoon he'd managed to ferret out the incident where Johnny Baker had kicked Tiger in the shin, what kind of lunches the school served, what Tiger did after school, that Mrs. Redding was probably the most beautiful teacher in the entire world. Sensitive to his father's moods, Tiger had grown tense and unhappy when he perceived Griff's displeasure over Sheila's manipulations. Griff didn't subdue his emotions for his son—neither his anger nor his love. He kept in touch, physical touch, with the boy—a hug here, an easy brush of hand to shoulder there . . . The shared laughter had rung out in the yard, as Griff had turned boy to match his son's enthusiastic bug catching.

Susan knew the love Griff felt for Tiger equaled his feelings for Barbara and Tom. This afternoon had just been special, a chance to really see Griff love his role as father, to see how very much he really enjoyed his son.

But there had been more, something subtly different about Griff all afternoon, something beneath the laughter with his son. A fleeting flash of sadness and guilt in his eyes, as well as the openly expressed anger. For a man who usually showed his emotions, he kept the sadness and guilt well hidden . . . but then Susan had been an expert at hiding emotions all her life. His pain was simply something that she couldn't stand, all the more because he didn't even know those big dark eyes of his were haunted with it.

But less so. Less haunted now, as he touched her. She leaned over to press a kiss on his chin. "Griff."

"Mmm?"

"What are you doing?" Her eyes danced up to his, amused that he was doing such a good job of soaping her fingers for the fourth time.

"The cooties. That's what we used to call them in fifth grade. When you had to touch a bug—" He watched her face color, and chuckled. Laziness had overtaken that first intense surge of passion; he was glad. Susan was too much fun to play with to hurry anything. He could easily spend a year discovering the feel of her flesh under water, reveling in feminine slopes and hollows, in the way her soft lips parted just so . . . when he touched, just so. Those fish of hers, that halo of blue light illuminating her expressive features . . .

Griff had treated her to the McDonald's take-home dinner they had planned for themselves and Tiger so he could chat instead of cooking. As it was, Susan had spent the saved time hovering over *Minnesota Insects,* to Griff's thorough amusement. He knew damn well she would be bringing home *The Care and Feeding of Hamsters* from her store on Monday.

That, too, was Susan—not just the water nymph who was taking her turn at teasing now, brushing her heavy, warm breasts fleetingly against his chest as she scrubbed his very clean shoulder. He took the washcloth from her hand, dropped it, and gently draped his arms around her neck. "Susan. No one is expecting you to be den mother of the month, love."

"I didn't—"

"You were perfectly super with him. He's adored you from the first minute he laid eyes on you." Griff's lips twisted. "Naturally. He's my son; he has good taste. But don't think I didn't have the urge to land a solid hand on his backside during the rumpus over the red alligator shirts."

"Yes. I've noticed your tendencies toward violence, Griff," she said wryly. "You have a mean streak a mile long. Tiger's just terrified of you."

He took a nonviolent nip out of her shoulder as punishment for her teasing. Or maybe as punishment for other things. She was driving him out of his mind with her subtle little shifts and movements. Her slim thighs cradled his hips; his flesh was already hot from the silken water, yet the heat in his loins was a different quality entirely.

"I know so little about children, Griff."

"You know everything about loving people. A four-foot-tall boy is no more sacred than a six-foot-tall man, Susie." He tilted her chin up. "Listen to me. I love you . . . for understanding. For being willing to have the kids with us. I want you to love them. But they're not perfect, no more so than any other children. And I don't want you to be afraid to tell me your feelings, or to be angry with them—"

"Griff—"

"And there are many, many times when I have no desire whatsoever to think about my kids. As in, skip the children for now. Let's talk about the house. About a canoe trip up north. About businesses—yours and mine. About logging. About how much I love you. About how damn much I want you at this minute."

She looked at him for one long, endless moment, then twisted her hips, just slightly. And surged forward, wrapping her legs even more tightly around him as she heard his startled release of breath, as she felt her whole body violently tremble at the sensation of the man inside her. Her eyes closed helplessly. The water made it . . . different. The soft, smooth water lapping around them stirred the most sensual messages, while the almost painful thrust of his arousal stirred others. She suddenly felt as limp as a kitten, and her eyes fluttered open again. Her lips parted slightly, needing that quick intake of air, needing to let it out again. "Is this what you wanted to talk about?" she murmured. "Or maybe you wanted to start with the house, Griff . . . ?"

"The lady," he growled, "is certainly a great deal more aggressive than when I first knew her." His lips hovered one teasing moment over her own. "Do you know how good you feel?" he murmured. "All tight and warm. Your skin has an extraordinary luster, and I can feel you trembling, Susan . . ."

Slippery hands stole slowly around her back under the water, pulling her that much closer, arching her spine as his mouth settled on hers. Her soft lips parted, inviting the sweet invasion of his tongue. The taste was pure Griff, the suction he created an echo of the hunger she could feel vibrating through his entire body. There was no haunted look in his eyes now, no memories of pain intruding on the emotions she saw in his face.

She drew up her legs an inch. There was no more

room than that. His thighs, trying to tighten around her, had no more room either. "Dammit," he muttered.

"Yes, Griff." She was soaring. His lips had turned feverish, intensely feverish, on her throat. He came back up for air, and that strange blue light illuminated the almost savage beauty of his features. His look of passion was so ardent that she could feel goose bumps rising on her flesh. *When* was she going to stop feeling like a virgin to his pirate?

A tiny flicker of danger hissed through her bloodstream whenever his mouth settled on hers and didn't let go. Danger . . . she never feared that he would hurt her, but she sensed that the power he held over her was as primitive as the oldest male-female battles. Griff was the stronger, his flesh smooth as metal, his rough, drugging kisses demanding her own response . . .

"Please . . ." she murmured.

His hands slid between them, grazing her stomach, sliding up to lift both breasts from the water. The valley between them glistened with droplets; water streamed over the satin orbs, so heavy in his hands. He bent to taste, but his lips would reach only so far without his breaking the melding of their lower bodies. Not for heaven or hell would he break that union. Frustration sent a single low growl from the back of his throat. He wrapped his arms around her, loving the feel of silken slipperiness where his chest rubbed against her more tender skin, and he rocked her, his face buried in the hollow of her neck, his lips dipping into every inch of her sensitive skin.

"Susan," he whispered roughly.

"Hmmm." She arched back, welcoming his kiss as she would welcome the warmth of sunlight. His teeth teased at her lower lip, and his tongue slipped inside her mouth again. Then out.

"Why the hell didn't you warn me ahead of time that the tub was too small?" he growled unfairly.

She smiled, but barely had time to comment before he reluctantly withdrew from her. In seconds, she was encouraged to stand on legs that had the tensile strength of marshmallows. Griff flicked open the drain, then surged up out of the water like some streaming bronzed giant; he hastily brushed a towel over himself, and another swallowed her up; then he lifted her, higher, higher...

She felt like booty to his pirate as he swung her out of that luminous light and carried her through the chilled black hall. He paused only once, as if suddenly realizing that her face was totally covered by the towel. His chin nudged it aside. Gray eyes flecked with silver were waiting for him, still drugged by their sensual play, but dancing just a little. He brushed a quick kiss on the tip of her nose. "We're getting a new bathtub," he murmured. "A larger one."

"Are we?"

He took three and a half seconds to dry them both off, then cool skin met cool skin: a new game. The mattress yielded to their combined weights, and all Susan could think was, Hurry, hurry. Nothing had ever felt so good as his full length against hers; the first rush of freedom to stretch and slide around him exploded a frantic desire within her. It wasn't really her, of course. Susan was reserved, wary of intimacy... It was all Griff's fault. From the very beginning, he'd cut through her shyness with a silken machete...

Moonlight suddenly played light and shadow on his face as Griff loomed over her. His own black-dark eyes on fire, he saw the soft, vulnerable gray eyes beneath his. Her skin was moist and seemed to glow in the dark. Firm, supple breasts ached against his chest, already well loved, cheek roughened, and comforted with his tongue and lips. Her whole body talked to him: He knew her ribs, the slim span of her waist, the incredible erotic tension that could grip her thighs when a passion was released in her that she still didn't understand...

They had years to go. Each time they loved, he had a searing need to show her that. She was so full of love; she gave and gave, yet always expected so little in return.

Her heart was pounding against his, her hands roving

his back in increasingly restless movements. "Griff," she murmured desperately.

He wasted no more time, taking her with exactly the sweet, fierce momentum she was asking for. Abandonment was her goal; she wanted only to present him with her richness, with a love he wanted to return to her tenfold. Her spine arched beneath him, and he cradled the shuddering explosion that took her body, a release all silver and satin, the essence of his life inside her.

Griff rested on his side. Beneath the comforter, he still held Susan captive, her warmth something he refused to let go of yet, even for sleep. Her tousled hair looked like dark satin on the pillow, and his callused palm smoothed the sleek strands back, loving the serene, smooth beauty of her face after loving.

Her hands were nestled between them, one palm resting over his heartbeat, waiting for it to slow to normal. "Can you tell me about it now?" she asked softly.

He kissed her forehead. "Tell you about what, lovely one?"

She propped herself up, leaning on one elbow, and slowly stroked the hair back from his forehead before she tried to speak. "You were different this afternoon, Griff. Unhappy. Closed in a way you've never seemed before. I'm supposed to be the inhibited one in this relationship, remember?"

His dark eyes glinted up at her. "Not so that you'd notice," he said gravely.

But she saw the quick, bleak sadness that touched his eyes again, and she didn't smile in return. "What's wrong, Griff?" she insisted quietly. "You're so good with Tiger. He adores you. He's a well-adjusted little bundle of energy . . ."

She waited, patiently. Griff was silent for a long time, but she could see the sudden tension in his profile by moonlight, in the eyes that darted away from her, in the tightness that was so rarely a part of him. Her perception came from feminine instincts that pursued him into those dark corners where he crouched away from her. Gently, her fingers stroked the furrow between his eyebrows.

"None of them took the divorce well," he said finally. "Tiger's the most resilient, but it hit him at a vulnerable time, too."

She stroked, over and over, her touch lighter than a feather.

"I have *always* been against divorce where children are concerned," he said flatly. "Maybe you make mistakes, even as an adult, but don't, for godsake, take them out on innocents. The marriage had been wrong for years, but the kids didn't know it. There were no arguments in front of them."

"And you still feel guilty as hell," she whispered.

"I *am* guilty as hell," Griff corrected. He shifted a pillow behind himself and moved up; she knew he moved to avoid her touch. There were certain kinds of pain he was used to bearing alone. And in response to that, she shifted with him, pushing her pillow up, keeping her hand on his arm.

"Try telling me about her," she suggested.

"Sheila?"

No, the lady in the moon. Susan was already too sensitive about his ex-wife, yet she knew Griff needed to say certain things out loud. He had coaxed her out of her own defensive shells, and she would coax him from his. "Just tell me," she insisted.

"What do you want to know?"

"Talk, Griff."

The muscle in his jaw flexed when he turned his head on the pillow. Dark eyes glittered on her softer gray ones. At this moment, Griff was not so very pleased with his too-perceptive wife. "She's a good-looking woman," he said flatly.

"That hurts. Naturally. Go right ahead, but when you're all through—"

Aaah. He gathered her close, shutting her up, burying her face in his shoulder, arching a leg around her to drag her nearer yet. He kissed her hard on her temples, and Susan relaxed, silent, waiting.

"We married too damn young," he admitted finally. "Sheila had been raised to 'catch a man.' That was the game. So she loved campfires and kids and quiet evenings, because those were the things I loved. Until she got the ring on her finger. Then she was so damned unhappy..." He took a breath. "Restless all the time. Moody with the kids, taking on causes with incredible enthusiasm, flitting from one thing to another...I don't know what she wanted from me. I never knew. Oh ...money, of course. The Anderson name..."

Susan wound her arms around his waist and snuggled closer, wanting desperately to cushion him from some of those memories. How many years had Griff been without love? But she knew, every time he touched her.

"For the kids, I kept trying. There was no love between Sheila and me, but I had the kids' love, and the five of us were surviving. Until Sheila stepped out with someone else. Then something just clicked inside me, an awareness of how little I really did care. From that point on, I just couldn't pretend with her anymore."

He took a breath. "We called it 'irretrievable breakdown of a marriage.' I never mentioned adultery in court; neither of us wanted to sling the kids through that kind of mud. But Sheila, for some reason, balked at the end and wanted the marriage to stand. The big fight came when we were talking custody in front of the judge. I wanted the kids, and I knew that she really didn't. She was just worried that people might say she was a bad woman and a terrible mother if she didn't fight for the kids. Maybe I could have won custody if I'd mentioned her affair to the judge. At the time, all I could think of was that we were hurting the children enough without bringing that up. I knew I'd claim my share of time with them, and since I had to work all week anyway and they were in school—"

"Which is all true, Griff," Susan interjected.

His jaws clamped together and then relaxed slightly.

"She doesn't love them. She never did. She loves the child-support money, but she's still off and running twelve hours of the day, never there. I've been back to my lawyer countless times, but there's nothing I can take to court. I can't prove she's done anything that shows her to be an unfit parent. Hers isn't the kind of neglect that shows... There was a time when I even felt sorry for her. She's incapable of loving anyone. Even herself. But the point is what she's doing to *them*—the kids. Tiger and Barbara and Tom. And *I'm* the one who initiated the divorce proceedings, who tore their lives apart."

"*Listen* to me." Susan extricated herself from his hold, and leaned up on one elbow to glare at him. "You haven't done anything wrong," she said furiously. "You love those kids like hell; you give them so much of yourself. Surely you don't think you're the only divorced father in this country? You know so many kids who've had a perfect, ideal upbringing? Your kids have had it a little tough, Griff, but they've never suffered from lack of care, lack of love, lack of anything they needed from you. It's the tough times that build character... or can build it. And don't you ever tell me you didn't have the right to fight for your own needs, dammit."

She was a cougar in the wild, so fierce in her defenses, so furious when her own were attacked... Griff sighed, feeling something released inside him that had been locked up for a very long time. In the four years since the divorce, he'd never discussed or even admitted to himself any of the lingering guilt he felt about it. Susan was somehow his mentor. Minx, mentor... lover, wife...

He turned, rearranged Susan's pillow, and dragged her down and flat beneath him, smiling into her startled eyes. In a tough business world, he inspired respect; he knew that. Even a little fear. A few people even jumped when he walked into a room, and no one had scolded Griff Anderson in at least two decades.

Except Susan, who could barely shoo away a fly without worrying about having done the creature harm.

"I love you, Susan," he told her tenderly.

The fires in her eyes softened as if cooled by a gentle rain. "I love you, too."

"Yes. Well. I don't want you starting any more nonsense like those acrobatics in the bathtub," he said sternly. His lips dipped down to taste the hollow between her shoulder and neck. A most vulnerable hollow. "And just a few days ago, there was that episode on the new dining room carpet." Edging lower, his palm gently cradled her right breast. Susan's breath suddenly caught when his tongue touched down. *"Hours* before that, you wanted to christen the kitchen. Susan, we are *never* again going to try to make love in a kitchen. Any kitchen..."

So very, very stern. *"Griff."* She could not possibly be feeling the renewal of fire again. Her head was spinning with Griff's memories, still. Her own insecurities, which Tiger's visit had triggered, had faded in a renewed understanding of why and how much Griff wanted his children with him. Beyond that, she was annoyed with Griff for harboring unnecessary guilt. All those emotions from the heart... yet her breasts went strangely taut under his lazy ministrations.

He suddenly turned them both on their sides, his brown eyes meeting hers in the dark room—full of the devil. Not to mention the devil's advocate pressed deliberately against her stomach. "You knew when we married that I was more than a decade older than you," he continued with mock gravity. "I hope you outgrow this... insatiable tendency of yours, Susan. I simply can't keep this up. Just because you have this irresistible, luscious little body..."

She lifted up her body and planted her lips on his. There was obviously a time for soul-searing discussions as well as a time... to give in. She'd wanted credit for the kitchen episode, anyway. And tomorrow was Sunday. They could nap all afternoon.

5

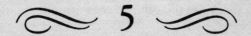

AS SUSAN SAT across the dinner table from Barbara, she was rather startlingly aware of how different the fourteen-year-old was from her gregarious younger brother. A week had passed since Tiger's brief visit. Susan and Griff had packed up the whole brood and taken them out to dinner on Wednesday; his ex-wife had raised no objection, even though it wasn't their "assigned time." Barbara had been distinctly cool that evening, though no one else seemed to notice. Susan had scolded herself that she was just *looking* to make mountains out of molehills as a result of her fear that the girl wouldn't accept her, but she wasn't making any mountains now as she and Barbara ate dinner alone together. Passing the plate of ham, she felt the tense silence between them. Someone at the table was sending out distinctly hostile messages. It wasn't Susan.

Tall and slim, Barbara had rich sable hair, worn long with a heavy fringe of bangs. Most teenagers would have killed for that porcelain complexion. Barbara was a beauty, give or take the adolescent garb. Newly budding breasts were concealed under a voluminous old sweat shirt; the jeans, by contrast, undoubtedly took her a half-hour to get out of; she had probably put them on wet and let them dry. The only feature of Griff's that Barbara had inherited was a pair of beautiful dark eyes, accented—five minutes after her father had left the house—with four coats of mascara.

Those eyes kept darting over to Susan, slipping past her favorite dinner, dancing past Susan's utterly innocuous gray wool pants and bright red sweater, glancing into Susan's compassionate gray eyes, flitting around the dining room, taking in the deacon's bench and long oak table and crystal chandelier . . . and apparently disdaining all of it.

Susan made every effort to send over her own share of silent messages: Honey, I'm sorry Griff isn't here; you know how much he values time with you. Yes, I know the last thing you want is to be stuck here alone with me. I've seen all those intimidating looks you keep giving me, but I'm not raising any white flags yet. And, yes, you little vixen, I've noticed the eye shadow and mascara, but you're going to have to wait until hell freezes over before I make any comments about the appropriate age at which to wear makeup. First of all, I have no interest in playing Wicked Stepmother, and second, if I'd had an asset like those big, beautiful eyes I would probably have worn mascara when I was five. Perhaps not *quite* that thick, but . . .

"Want some chocolate cake?" Susan stood up with her plate in her hand.

"No, thank you," Barbara said stiffly.

Susan juggled a few more dishes in her arms before heading toward the kitchen, ignoring Barbara's glacial voice. "Your dad said he'd call around eight. Barbara, you know he had no idea until four this afternoon that he was going to be anywhere but right here with you. It wasn't his fault that—"

"You told me."

"He's still hoping to be here by noon tomorrow."

"Sure." Barbara unfolded her long legs from under the table, a very odd mixture of feminine grace and early teenage clumsiness. She followed Susan, taking no dishes, and stood in the doorway while her stepmother started storing the leftovers. "Dad's probably just as happy anyway. Like I was expecting something like this. A setup, you know?"

Susan turned startled eyes to her. "What are you talking about?"

"Oh, come on, Susan. Here we are, *getting to know each other*. I mean, like you're supposed to be part of *my* family now, too, right? So you're taking us on, one at a time. First Tiger, now me. Then Tom."

Susan closed the refrigerator with a little thump, well aware what the girl thought of that particular program. An elephant couldn't have missed the sarcasm. She ran the sink full of hot water and added enough soap to wash the dishes forty times over. "It's rough for you, isn't it?" She briskly put the dishes into the sink. "You were used to having a lot of private time with your dad. Naturally, you're afraid I'm going to cut into that and interfere in your relationship with him in other ways, too. On top of that, of course, you have a mother already; you don't need two. I think if I were in your shoes, I'd feel just as uptight as you do." She added casually, "I don't mind washing, but I hate drying."

Barbara's stricken look might or might not have resulted from her resentment at being expected to dry the dishes, but she took up the towel anyway. Silence returned like an unwanted friend. Susan thought with wry desperation that she must have scored at least a minor hit; what fun is it to attack an enemy who won't fight back? The silence was no fun, either, though.

For Susan, the worst part of being stared at was that she couldn't dry her hands and finish off the single fingernail she'd started unobtrusively biting five minutes after Barbara walked in. Having beaten the horrible habit when she was fifteen, Susan suddenly clearly remembered what it felt like to have a half-gnawed nail that craved to be evened up.

Griff called a few minutes later from Duluth, only to tell them he couldn't possibly be home until late Sunday morning. He talked to his daughter for more than twenty minutes, while Susan finished the dishes, desperately missed her husband, and sweated out how on earth she was going to entertain Barbara for two evenings and an entire day.

"Darling, is it going all right?" he asked Susan when his daughter finally handed her the phone.

"Just fine," she told him blithely.

As they walked out of the kitchen a few minutes later, Barbara complained, "I don't understand what's so important to Dad about that stupid land, anyway. It's not like it's worth anything. Mom told me ages ago that all the real money comes from the plants in St. Paul. There's no reason why Dad still has to go up there all the time."

"It's the land your great-grandfather homesteaded," Susan answered. And that he destroyed, Griff had told her. He and the others of his generation pillaged the forests, and no one had thought to replant them until thirty years ago. Griff's father had planted jack pine, a tree that grew fast enough to provide a regular income, yet Griff had different dreams for the land. He was meeting forestry people over the weekend. Busy people, like him. There was no other time.

"So what does that have to do with anything?" Barbara insisted petulantly. "If it doesn't make money, what's the point of it?"

Susan sighed. It wasn't the first time she'd felt like giving Griff's ex-wife a good kick in the chops for engraining in her offspring such a materialistic attitude. "The love of the forest is the point," she said patiently.

Barbara seemed momentarily diverted as she started roaming from room to room. Susan followed, hoping the girl would find some of the spirit of "home" that she and Griff saw in the house. Everything wasn't done, of course. They'd hurried through the big jobs, the repairing and painting and tearing up that were needed to make the house livable. Tiger's and then Barbara's room had been Susan's top priorities, and the downstairs was still skimpily furnished. But there was enough, surely, so that Barbara could see that the goal was comfort and space? A place she might want to come home to...

The girl paused at the threshold to the library. Russet carpet led up to the small fire Susan had laid in the hearth. The bookshelves were filled now, and Griff's antique maps hung on the walls; the silver sconces above the fireplace had been polished, and they gleamed in the firelight. Nubby cream-colored couches faced each other; their cushions begging to be sunk into. Where Griff had uncovered the treasure, Susan didn't know, but he'd converted a small semicircular gaming table into a writing desk; its dark patina shone in contrast to the original oak paneling and the rich russet of the new carpet.

"Mom likes blue," Barbara remarked.

"I'm sure she does."

Barbara subjected the living room to the same intense scrutiny. "You *are* going to get some furniture sooner or later, aren't you? I mean, not just this old stuff?"

Susan stuffed her hands in her pockets. The living room was rather empty still. The two Oriental rugs were her pride and joy. Her six-legged French desk, an exquisite eighteenth-century corner chair, a Sak sideboard, and yes, a rather dilapidated old couch, because they really hadn't had the time to shop for what they wanted. Still, Susan loved this room, from its high ceiling to the old-fashioned transoms to the circular, leaded-glass windows with the built-in seats beneath. Obviously, Sheila favored more contemporary styles and had passed her tastes on to her daughter. "Would you like to see your room?" Susan asked helplessly.

Barbara hesitated momentarily at the foot of the stairs, staring back into the living room and then inscrutably at Susan. "It is kind of an interesting old house," she admitted.

"Thank you. We think so, too," Susan said dryly.

Barbara flashed her a look. No, Susan told herself, don't risk any more ironic comments.

Susan held her breath while Barbara climbed the stairs ahead of her and found the way to her room. She'd worried about that room more than any other. At fourteen, Susan had been miserable or insecure herself

. . . probably no more miserable or insecure than any other adolescent, but she hadn't found that out until later. Rebellion, anxiety, ambivalence, parents—everything had seemed dreadful at that age. Susan remembered, and had hoped to say so much to Barbara with this room . . .

The bed was a Jenny Lynn, its graceful lines accented by a pale blue comforter. The corner under the window had begged for a little dressing table; Susan had sewed the skirt herself, light blue with mauve, to match the curtains. The desk was blue with gold trim, the carpeting more expensive per yard than the russet in the library. The closet was ample, but Susan had fallen in love with an old wardrobe and antiqued it in white, with just a hint of blue at the edges.

This room was pretty enough to make up for having to go through adolescence. Susan had done the best she could . . .

Barbara turned to her, suddenly all dark eyes like her father's. "I never asked you to do anything like this."

"I know."

"I . . ." Barbara turned back to the room that had been so lovingly prepared for her. "It's a pretty special bedroom," she said grudgingly.

Susan felt as if she'd just finished a snifter of champagne. Champagne was not served in snifters. Which was completely irrelevant.

Twenty-four hours later, the doorbell rang for the umpteenth time. Running a hand distractedly through her dark hair, Susan ran to answer it. She blinked hard at the three grinning boys on the porch steps, her brilliant smile unwavering as she let them in. Finding the President standing on the doorstep would not have surprised her at this point.

Barbara had talked her into giving an impromptu party. A few friends, though, seemed to have snowballed into a multitude. All girls, Susan had so naively assumed. Clearly not the case, although given the hairstyles and unisex clothing, it was sometimes hard to tell.

Sheila evidently didn't allow parties, simply because she was rarely at home to chaperon them. Susan had known damn well that Barbara was testing her, but there didn't seem to be a valid reason not to let the girl have her way. They'd been doing so well since Barbara had seen her room. How much trouble could a few girl friends be? Griff wasn't there to be annoyed by the noise or debris. And all day she and Barbara had had a good time together, fixing snacks, going to the store to buy soft drinks and potato chips. Barbara had unpacked Griff's stereo, looked through the records... They had made another trip to buy more suitable albums. Griff relaxed to Tchaikovsky; his daughter relaxed to the Screaming Meemies. Or a variation thereof.

That was fine, but Susan had clearly not anticipated the rest of the evening. At fourteen, Susan had been into pajama parties, potato chips, and rereading the love scenes from *Gone with the Wind*.

Barbara was doing a wild dance in the living room that made Susan blush. So were a dozen others. Some of them were old enough to drive cars... and had rather sophisticated ideas about entertainment. The music was mind-blowing, a phrase Susan suddenly understood very well. Since there was only one lamp in the living room, the light was rather muted. There was a couple on the couch who hadn't... let up... in an hour.

After ushering in the three newcomers, Susan hurried back to the kitchen, poured potato chips into yet another bowl, hurriedly whipped up some fresh dip, and frantically tried to gather her thoughts. She could hardly have missed the belligerent looks Barbara had flashed at her over the last two hours, looks that said, *Go ahead, Susan;* come on like the Green Berets; it's just what I expect from you...

So there were two youngsters necking on the couch. And the rest were dancing as if it were some primitive mating ritual. So there were three dozen instead of a nice, manageable six...

At fourteen, even after having been handed all the

appropriate books, Susan had really not been absolutely positive that babies didn't come from belly buttons. She realized that she was now looking into the depths of a massive generation gap. A shy, demure bookworm had no comprehension of "letting it all hang out."

She was trying. Maybe not hard enough, though, because the sight of two teenagers petting on the couch shocked her. When she was fourteen, she would never have allowed a boy to touch those very new, very sensitive, very small breasts she'd waited so long for nature to develop. *Dammit.* To touch like that in front of three dozen other people...

What exactly was she supposed to do? *Not* fail Griff, she told herself. He was so worried about Barbara, so convinced she needed a mature yet feminine woman to talk to her...and Barbara was not going to listen to anyone who came on like a police patrol.

Pushing the kitchen door open with her hip, Susan carried the tray of chips and dip into the dining room, a smile fixed on her face that made the muscles in her cheeks ache. The two boys perched on the windowseat looked startled when she came in, then smiled just as brilliantly back at her. Fortunately, her eyes were quicker than the boys' hands. She saw the brown paper bag they tried to hide, and she smelled the beer. "I have Coke," she told them brightly.

"That's okay. We're not thirsty, Mrs. Anderson."

"Oh, I'm sure you are." She whipped the tray onto the table; she delivered two Cokes from the kitchen. Hastily, she popped the tops and forced the cold cans into the boys' hands. Susan perched on the seat next to them, prepared to chat. When the two boys fled to join the others, in predictable horror at having to talk to an adult, she claimed the brown-bagged booty and buried it in the trash, almost before her stomach had developed an ulcer.

The victory was minor; her nose led her to other trouble. Barbara's eyes were riveted to hers yet again as

Susan passed through the living room. Anxious, troubled eyes? But by now Susan doubted her own perceptions where Barbara was concerned. At any rate, there was the strangest smell . . .

She paused in the doorway to the library, watching a boy light up a joint and pass it to a girl, who took a drag and then handed it to another boy. Plain cigarettes would have been bad enough; the kind those three kids were smoking knotted another ball of panic in Susan's stomach. She saw the flicker of ash on her brand-new carpet and had had enough. She would have to win over Griff's daughter another time. Striding over to the troublemakers with a brilliant smile, she snatched the marijuana cigarette away from the third smoker, watched three mouths drop in shock at her sudden appearance, and tossed the offending reefer into the fire. "Do you have a ride home?" she asked them pleasantly.

That seemed to start a roller coaster in her brain that refused to slow down. She sped back to the living room, avoiding Barbara's eyes and swooped down on the boy and girl who were necking. "Would you like some potato chips and dip?" she suggested brightly.

The girl flushed crimson; the boy just stared at her as if she were out of her mind.

"You *would* like some potato chips and dip," Susan said firmly. *"Now."*

Outside there was a noise. The sprawling old elm was climbable, unfortunately. At least the swinging monkeys more closely resembled what Susan remembered fourteen-year-olds to be. She shooed them down, went back inside to serve one last round of hot dogs, and took two aspirin. Then, acting on a sudden hunch, she raced upstairs to find another adolescent couple looking for a place to fool around.

Over and over during the melee she caught Barbara's eyes on hers, still belligerent yet somehow pleading and desperately unhappy. Barbara had never left the dance floor; in fact, Griff's daughter had never been part of the disasters that had been going on. Barbara hadn't been smoking or necking or drinking . . . but as for the friends her mother evidently allowed her to socialize with . . .

"Look, Susan," Barbara said miserably some hours after the party had ended, "I'll clean everything up."

Susan was on her knees, as was Barbara, both of them trying to remove a stain of unknown origin from the expensive Oriental rug. It was past midnight, and the house was suddenly quiet. Her lovely, lovely house, Susan lamented. Soda cans were everywhere, chips were deeply imbedded in the carpet, snacks were strewn about haphazardly, and water stains marked the newly varnished sideboards . . . Susan lifted her head and stared at Barbara, then picked up the soaked towels and stood up, snatching up assorted soda cans on her way back to the kitchen.

Susan was hurt, and close to tears. Barbara trailed silently after her, carrying so many cans that a few tumbled to the floor, making a terrible racket. Barbara's head jerked up, her eyes still guiltily expecting a tongue-lashing from her new stepmother.

It didn't happen. Susan simply picked up the last of the debris and then hauled out the vacuum cleaner. She was certainly not going to let Griff come home to this mess; she didn't care what time it was. Barbara stayed in the kitchen, having filled the sink with soapy water without even being asked to do so.

Susan pushed the noisy vacuum cleaner over every inch of the new carpets, ignoring wet spots, not particularly caring if she got electrocuted. Her head ached; her back was feeling the strain of the long day . . . but it was her heart that felt torn to pieces. The hurt came from knowing that she'd been so naive as to be set up by one fourteen-year-old child. It came from the hours she'd spent painting and furnishing Barbara's room, anticipating that a slow but sure course of honest affection and gentleness would win the girl over, a naive belief that if she went 90 percent of the way, Barbara would surely come the other 10 percent.

Yes, Barbara was unhappy, guilty, and miserable now. Maybe she hadn't expected things to get quite so out of hand, but Susan was almost certain that Barbara was panicking with fear that Susan would tell Griff about the party. Barbara's remorse was not really regret for what she'd put Susan through. She couldn't have gone more out of her way to totally reject her father's wife...

Finally after going over the carpet four times, Susan turned the vacuum cleaner off. As she was winding the chord, she glimpsed Barbara from the corner of her eye, hugging the wall by the door, her face pasty-white and her eyes stricken.

In spite of herself, and in spite of every rational instinct she'd ever possessed, Susan felt an unwelcome surge of compassion. "Barbara, it's all right. Just go to bed," she said quietly. "It's all over."

"Like I didn't know some of those guys. They were older. The thing was, the kids I invited needed someone older to drive them to this side of town, but I didn't—"

However true that was, Susan knew the party had been planned to convey to her exactly what Barbara thought of her stepmother. Pushing a strand of hair back from her cheek, Susan straightened up from winding the vacuum chord. "The two boys you seemed to spend most of your time dancing with," Susan said casually. "They looked like nice kids..."

"Steve is." Barbara hesitated. "Those guys that pushed their way in were creeps. Crashers. None of the girls I go around with have anything to do with Barry..."

Barbara was so busy covering her tracks, yet Susan heard the grain of truth. It mattered, because she needed to hear that Barbara didn't normally associate with certain of those teenagers before she could promise silence, something she knew Barbara was desperate to hear.

She pushed the vacuum cleaner into the closet and

closed the door. "I don't think we need to tell your father," she said quietly.

Barbara's face promptly took on a little color.

"It was between you and me, anyway, wasn't it?" Susan said sadly. "Go to bed, Barbara. It's late."

The girl lost no time racing up the stairs. Susan couldn't possibly have told her that she had no desire to inform Griff for her own sake; that she couldn't bear to let him know how badly she had bungled her attempt to establish a relationship with the child he loved so dearly. She almost felt like laughing. She'd thought she had so much to share with his only daughter; she could remember so well how tough it was to be that age, that blend of grace and clumsiness, that special insecure person a fourteen-year-old girl was. Her total lack of experience with children had troubled her, but she had thought that at least with Barbara, despite the tough exterior...

First, bugs with Tiger, and now rebellion from Barbara... Susan mounted the stairs with a feeling of despair. She'd known before she married Griff that his kids were part of the package; with so much love inside her, she'd welcomed the challenges she'd known were coming.

It had just never occurred to her before that she could totally fail.

6

AN HOUR AND a half later, the lights were off, the house was silent, and Susan was in bed . . . very definitely *not* sleeping. Myriad troubled thoughts bounced back and forth in her mind. How *could* she have made such a swift, foolish promise to Barbara not to tell Griff about the party? He had a right and a need to know what his daughter was up to, and there was something all wrong with a marriage in which the wife kept secrets from her husband.

At the same time, though, Susan knew there was absolutely no way she could break trust with Barbara, tentative though that trust was. Over and over, she analyzed Barbara's attitude. One cup teenage insecurity, one cup a dominant mother's jealous preaching. Mix well. Stir in a loving father who pulled the girl in yet another direction; sift in peer influences and suddenly whip in an unknown woman who could so unfairly add a few more rules and expectations to confuse an already baffled teenager. It was really no surprise that the pie wouldn't bake.

Susan desperately wanted to tell Griff that she was afraid she was failing two out of three of his children. She craved his reassurance that he didn't expect an instant love affair between her and his offspring, that he understood these were just the first rounds. She still had faith that she could win Barbara over eventually. But it was difficult to take a long-term perspective when the clock was happily ticking toward three o'clock in the morning. Fears and insecurities thrived at that hour.

She adored Griff. She had no doubts that he loved her, but who was kidding whom? He would never have married a woman who didn't love his kids. Well, she *did* love his children. She would love to take the dark-eyed Barbara in her arms and hug all that tension and insecurity away; she would willingly try to become a football star for Tiger. Instead . . .

Shut it off, Susan. Turn the pillow to the cool side; you've fretted over everything right down to the crossed *t*'s; now stop analyzing. She closed her eyes determinedly, only to hear a muffled thud from below. Her eyes opened wide in the darkness yet again, but she didn't move. She was too good a friend of insomnia not to know that an overtired, anxious brain could invent noises in the night.

A carpeted step creaked, and her heart promptly went into high gear, pumping a surplus of adrenaline. Pushing back the comforter, she suddenly remembered with brilliant clarity that she hadn't locked the back door. And that Barbara's room was even more vulnerable than hers to an intruder.

As she skimmed barefoot over the icy floor and into the hall, Susan heard another creak at the top of the stairs. It was pitch-black, impossible to see a thing. One hand groped, trying to find the wall . . . and collided with a different kind of wall entirely. Buttons and flannel. English leather. A low, throaty chuckle sent the anxious ghosts whispering back to the attic, as firm, warm hands steadied her bare shoulders.

"What on *earth* are you still doing up?" Griff whispered. "Susan, you're freezing . . ."

Not for long. Before she could begin to scold him for terrifying her, he scooped up her slim body and snuggled her close to himself. She luxuriated in the feel of Griff, his solid strength and warmth, the sheer, sprawling male of him. Surely he'd been away a year?

"Did I frighten you?" he whispered. "Coming in so late, I was trying to be as quiet as a mouse." With an arm still around her shoulder, he led her toward the bedroom. "God, I missed you," he murmured. "I knew it was a mistake not to take you with me, Susan. I couldn't sleep all last night."

His kiss, so swift and hard, slowed up all the blood in Susan's veins, and encouraged her to feel limp and weak. "I missed you, too," she admitted.

He patted her rear end, nudging her toward the bed, and started taking off his shirt, not bothering to turn on the light. He could see by moonlight all that he wanted to look at: the wisp of satin and lace that clung alluringly to Susan's magnolia skin, the silky cap of curls all tousled around her cheeks, the grace of her long legs in motion, and the velvet-gray of her eyes as she gazed at him . . .

"The manager of the motel must have thought I was crazy," he whispered as he turned to the closet to hang up his pants. "I checked in at eight-thirty and then out again an hour later. I should have called you then, Susan. I knew there was no point in my trying to sleep there."

In the luminous glow of moonlight that spilled into the room, Susan caught a glimpse of the weary shadows beneath his eyes, a white-gray tiredness on his face that she didn't like at all. "Griff, did everything go all right?"

"It went fine. Except that I kept thinking you should be there, breathing in the scent of the pines. You've been working so damn hard in this house, Susan. We both have, and it's not as though there's a rush. At least for one long weekend, we've got to take a trip up north this fall."

Griff yawned sleepily as he scooted Susan over on the mattress and immediately dropped down next to her. "I want to make love with you," he murmured huskily. "I've been wanting to make love to you since five minutes after I left the house on Friday. Do you have any idea how good you feel?"

Susan obligingly slid closer to him, until their limbs were irretrievably tangled together, her cheek nestled against his bare chest. She suddenly felt warm again, reassured, well loved . . . and sleepy. A sensual call whispered in her head, but she knew with affectionate amusement that it would have to wait until tomorrow, whatever Griff's intentions. His eyes were already closing.

"Did it go okay with Barbara?" he questioned groggily.

She barely hesitated. This wasn't the time for a discussion of her problems with his daughter. At any rate, no matter how much she regretted making the promise to Barbara . . . she *had* promised. "Fine."

He leaned over her one last time, his kiss sleepy and warm. "You didn't tell me if you realized how good you feel," he whispered teasingly. "Come closer."

She did.

"You smell like violets," he murmured, and fell asleep.

With a frown, Griff rose from his desk, snatched up the September bank statement he'd been working on, and went in search of Susan. After dinner, she'd retreated to the living room, surrounding herself with a cupful of tailor's tacks, yards of embossed material, scissors, and a newly refinished Queen Anne chair. The mess was still there, but Susan wasn't.

Nor was she upstairs, or in the kitchen. He stood there exasperated for a moment, noticing again the blazing flutter of gold leaves on the elms outside the window. That had happened almost overnight after an early October frost. On his trip north three weeks ago, the color change had not yet started . . . He heard a faint sound coming from the basement, strode to the cellar door, and took a few steps down; if he leaned over, he could see into the huge storage room.

She was there. On top of the dryer sat a small cage, and Susan was bending over it. In the pink ruffled blouse and cranberry skirt she'd worn to work, his wife looked alluringly feminine and distinctly unsuited to the task of cleaning an animal's cage. With a small sigh, he folded the sheet of paper in his hand and stuck it in his back pocket. He had been irritated with Susan a moment ago, but the determination to express his annoyance seemed to have vanished.

She winced suddenly and jumped back, away from the cage. Rapidly shaking her hand, she suddenly turned and spotted Griff halfway down the stairs. A guilty smile hovered on her lips. "Hi. I thought you were busy doing paper work."

"What on earth is that?"

"You mean the cage?" She motioned vaguely in the direction of the animal who'd just taken such a nasty little nip out of her finger. "That's a hamster for Tiger, a special type of hamster from Peru . . . or is it Venezuela? I was going to tell you about it when you were in a good mood." She peered up at him with dancing eyes. "Are you in a good mood?"

He was, she decided. Maybe a wee bit on the impatient side, but he'd had that kind of work week. She scampered up the stairs to offer him a kiss to make up for going against his wishes on the subject of hamsters. Her palms lingered unnecessarily long on his jeaned hips. She did like the look of Griff in jeans.

"You were right," she said cheerfully. "They smell terrible. The cage has to be cleaned all the time, and the little stinker bites. So if you *really* insist, I'll take him back where he came from. I just thought that Tiger would enjoy him. Especially since he's so much bigger and more colorful than plain old American hamsters, and so *fierce*."

She waited. Griff removed her hands from dangerous territory and placed them on his shoulders, bending his forehead to hers, "That meek, submissive line sounds pretty good," he growled.

"You like that?"

"I like that. I just can't imagine why I have the feeling

that you're going to keep the hamster no matter what I say."

Susan grinned. "But I'll be much smarter next time," she assured him.

He shook his head. "I doubt that." He trailed her lithe hips as they darted up the stairs ahead of him, a burst of love shooting through him as he watched her. Susan refused to acknowledge that she was doing too much and worrying too much about his kids. Take last night, when she'd dragged him outside to practice catching baseballs. His wife was not totally unathletic, but she had the worst depth perception of anyone he'd ever met. If they hadn't had so much fun laughing, he would have called her on her maternal worries then. Now just didn't seem to be the time.

"What are you up to for the moment?" he asked.

Susan made a vague motion in the direction of the living room and then huddled over the refrigerator. She poured them both fruit juice, added ice cubes, and handed Griff his glass. He understood her to mean that she wanted to finish reupholstering the Queen Anne chair. "You're doing too much," he complained. "Thirty more minutes, lady, while I finish my paperwork. Then we'll make a fire and warm some cider. Sound good?"

"Sounds very good," she agreed, as she sat down her glass. "What was wrong?" she asked curiously.

"What do you mean?"

"When you came downstairs to the basement, I had the feeling you were about to say something."

"I was." Griff sighed, having difficulty trying to dredge up the annoyance he had felt earlier. "Honey, you're still wearing jeans you had in high school; you suffer over every light bulb left burning in the house unattended; and if I remember correctly, you dragged me to a total of seven stores before you found an acceptable price for the carpeting in the library."

She remembered that shopping expedition. They'd had a terrific time, testing carpeting in their stockinged feet—obviously a major consideration, how carpeting felt on bare feet—as the salesman had ranted on about the number of fibers per square inch. "Are you tactfully trying to suggest I might be stingy with a dollar?"

"Tight as a fist. And on that basis, I'd normally invite you to overdraw the checking account any time, Susan. Actually, I was rather pleased to see you splurge..."

Wheels clicked in her head. Last weekend, Tom was supposed to finally make up his postponed weekend alone with them. He hadn't come—something about a party, although Susan was afraid the real reason Tom had canceled for the third time was more complex than the boy's unusually busy social schedule. He'd called her specially...but Tiger and Barbara had both come in his stead that weekend. Knowing a few days ahead about the change in plans, Susan had had the brilliant, impromptu idea of trying another time to take on Barbara in a one-on-one situation. "Actually, I spent a little money on Barbara," Susan admitted quietly, a troubled look in her eyes before she quickly reached for Griff's glass, to wash it out.

"Barbara?"

"I just forgot to tell you, Griff."

"Susan. My daughter has three times more clothes than you do, and since that episode with Tiger, you know damn well that each of my children has an adequate clothing allowance."

"More than adequate," Susan agreed, setting the clean glasses back in the cupboard. "And I certainly wasn't trying to buy her, Griff. But she wears such damn tight jeans, along with all the other faddish horrors she feels she needs to be popular with her crowd. And girls do like shopping, so I thought I could kind of subtly show her there were alternatives. You know. Being part of the crowd, but still keeping one's own sense of style." Susan hesitated, remembering all too well the shopping spree with Barbara. For a time, the excursion had seemed to go swimmingly...until Barbara saw a spangly T-shirt that seemed perfect...for a hooker. End of rapport. Susan glanced up at her husband, to find Griff's eyes intensely pinning hers, a frown grooved into his forehead.

"She's giving you a hard time, isn't she?" he demanded, very quietly.

"No."

"She's turned incredibly sassy since she became a teenager. Don't protect her, Susan. If she's giving you trouble—"

"She isn't," Susan denied emphatically, and willed sincerity to radiate from her clear gray eyes.

"We were so close when she was little. But after the divorce, she acted as if I had deserted *her*." He took a breath. "Her mother doesn't put any limits on her behavior. She just lets Barbara run free, and I've seen her becoming more and more spoiled. But at the same time..."

At the same time, he desperately wanted to give his daughter love, not discipline. Susan understood, so very clearly that she blinked back tears. No, she was not going to add to Griff's worries about his children by burdening him with her own. The thing to do, she'd decided weeks ago, was simply to try harder herself.

"Barbara will be fine," she assured him. "She's smart and pretty, and I haven't met a happy teenager yet, Griff. It's absolutely no fun being well adjusted when everyone else is suffering growing pains and has a wealth of trouble to complain about. She'll turn out fine."

Susan honestly believed that. The issue only became clouded when she thought of herself in relation to Griff's daughter. As she headed back to the living room, her upholstering project seemed a lesser priority. When Griff walked in a half-hour later, he found her ensconced on the couch with a book. That she was relaxing pleased him, though he was mildly surprised at the refuse of upholstery trimmings still scattered on the floor. Susan was normally a confirmed neatnik.

She murmured a greeting but didn't look up as Griff opened the flue of the fireplace and started stacking cherry logs on the andirons. He glanced back at her, perhaps unconsciously expecting her to join him. It was past nine.

It had been a long day away from her, in which he found himself frequently anticipating her smile, her lazy laughter, those private moments they shared in an evening.

She turned the page, but didn't look up. He struck a match and stayed crouched by the hearth until the flames were shooting up the chimney, then retreated to the kitchen to heat up a little cider. Mulled cider on a crisp evening with a hot little yellow fire glowing . . . Griff walked back into the living room with the two mugs; Susan murmured a protest when he set one down next to her, but didn't move.

Both amused and exasperated, Griff replaced the pillow under her head with his lap, rearranged her just a little so he knew her head and shoulders were comfortable, and watched her turn another page.

She was engrossed in *Tough Love,* a popular seller in the bookstore among adolescents' parents. The book's basic message was that a show of discipline was a show of love, that it was perfectly all right for a parent to say no, and that exercising control was probably tougher on the parent than it was on the child . . . It sounded so right . . . for a parent. But Susan was a stepparent.

With Tiger, Tough Love wasn't the issue. Balls were the issue—as in foot, base, and basket. Susan was a hiker and a canoer and a swimmer. Hand her a ball and she was lost. Griff found it very funny that she lacked depth perception; so did she. What difference did it really make? But it had made a difference last weekend when Tiger had totally given up playing with her because she couldn't catch a single ball.

But how could she say no to Barbara? The philosophy in the book was very appealing, but the writers weren't dealing with the stereotype of the Wicked Stepmother. Sheila gave Barbara no rules, and now Susan was supposed to jump in and convince Barbara that she was acting out of love? It wasn't just the spangled T-shirt. It was the sass she handed Susan behind Griff's back; it was worrying about whom the child was socializing with . . .

"Susan."

She tilted her head back, looking up at her husband gravely. "Listen. Do you have some sort of organized philosophy about the discipline of children?"

"God in heaven."

He confiscated the book, set down his glass of cider for the second time, and turned off the lamp over their heads. "We need to have a little talk," he informed her.

"Griff—"

He hauled her up just that little bit farther so she was sitting on his lap, a captive audience. "I think it's time I took you away from here."

"Away from here?"

"Honey, as much as I love them, I do not need to talk about my children every minute of the day. I just might even be interested in hearing what *you* did every minute of the day. Imagine that?" His mouth teased at her lower lip when she started to protest. "We're about to put the children on hold. And the house. And our work. And drop back five for a little solid time together. *Capisce?"*

He was the only Norwegian she knew who flaunted his sole Italian word. She answered in French, since that seemed to be the kind of kiss he was looking for.

7

SUSAN DIPPED HER paddle into the water once, then twice, finally lifting the dripping oar to let it rest across the gunwales of the canoe. Griff was leaning back against the bow, facing her, his legs stretched out and his ankles crossed, a hat tipped lazily over his forehead to block out the rays of the still-potent sun. The canoe made no sound as it traveled through the still, clear waters.

They'd been following the narrow stream all day. Like the lace of a spider's web, the maze of rushing water pivoted and curled in endless, intricate patterns. As they rounded a bend, Susan saw the trees that regally crowded the back of the stream. Birch and elm, aspen, maple, and locust, all arched for the sky, their leaves seemingly painted in brilliant fall colors. The late-afternoon sun glinted on apricot and scarlet, gold and russet. Not a leaf stirred, not a sound troubled the forest.

A mile farther upstream and another quarter-turn, suddenly huge boulders crowded the shore line, as though a giant had whimsically stashed his marbles in this private niche of northern Minnesota. Certainly no one would intrude on his treasures here. At a single splash of the canoe paddle, a dozen ducks would flutter skyward in alarm, honking and squawking at the first hint of an intruder.

One more mile, one more turn, and the stream widened slightly, its current growing swifter. Vertical cliffs jutted sharply up from the banks. A sharp eye could see a cave or the thin diamond spill of a waterfall, both possessively concealed by nature among foliage and rock.

"Tired?" Griff murmured.

"Impossible."

"Hungry, then?"

Susan was starving, but when she didn't answer, Griff raised his head to look at her, his eyes as warm as that lazy late sun. "You're the only woman I've ever known who's as greedy for this country as I am. You realize that you refused to stop for lunch?"

"*I* refused? You had the paddle at noon."

"You took over when I wanted to go ashore on that island."

"You were fed," Susan protested.

"Granola bars. Baby food."

The canoe rocked precariously when Susan tipped off his hat with her toe; then she had to pick up the paddle again or risk running into the streambank. They both fell silent, listening to the sudden mournful cry of a loon in the distance. Night was coming; the bird announced it.

Primitive wilderness, some called these boundary waters of the north; more water than land, thousands of acres completely inaccessible by car. A moose had made them laugh that morning; such a regal, magnificent half-ton of a beast, chomping on a mouthful of dripping weeds. Squirrels and foxes and beavers had posed on the stream-bank all day, too astonished at the sight of human intruders to be afraid. White-tailed deer had lapped thirstily at the crystal waters, bolting if the paddle made a splash.

Griff reached out toward her, and with a grin Susan handed him the paddle and watched him settle down to work. They didn't need words. Being alone with Griff had intensified that private communication they had, that feeling of love that didn't need explanations. His children had nothing to do with it, nor did her working life or his.

"Hear it?" Griff murmured.

The whispered gush of the rapids was a distance away,

but Susan couldn't mistake it. Already Griff was carefully shifting to a kneeling position. Sunlight glinted on his muscled forearms as he claimed a more definite grip on the paddle. "Susan..."

"Take it, Griff." All day they'd been searching for white water, a whim of Susan's. She'd always wanted to shoot a rapids. Shivering suddenly, she took up the second paddle. Their food and sleeping bags were sealed in plastic, well protected from a dunking. Adrenaline streaked through her blood as Griff sure-stroked silently, faster and faster, toward yet another bend in the stream.

Suddenly, ahead she could see whipped-cream foam on the water and the fast rush of silver around golden rocks in the sun.

"*Susan!* Hold on!"

But she already knew. The canoe lurched as it grazed a hidden rock and then surged forward in a downstream rush. The roar of fast water filled her ears; blinding sunlight flashed and faded among the tree limbs on the shore. White water splashed into the canoe, soaking both of them. Susan was freezing, gasping cold. Griff didn't have to tell her that the whispering sounds they'd heard a moment ago had been deceptive. One clumsy stroke and the canoe would capsize. One wrong move and they could crash into solid rock...

Danger sent excitement through her nerve endings. Excitement, but not fear. Griff was with her. Her hands clenched around the paddle; she stopped breathing, and her whole body jolted when another hidden boulder bounced the canoe, but those tremors of fear only heightened a sensual excitement greater than a roller-coaster ride. This was real, not play. This was *life*. Breathing. Being aware. Sound, touch, sight, even the taste of the sweet, icy water...

Laughter suddenly bubbled up inside her as she saw what Griff saw ahead. The white water ended in a scant two-foot cascade. Beyond it the stream was perfectly calm again. Even as she could see what was coming, she knew there was no way to avoid it. They were headed straight for the falls. Griff paddled valiantly, but they were just approaching at a speed too fast to control. The canoe careened through the air, hurtled smoothly into the quiet water below the cascade, and then unceremoniously flipped over and dumped its passengers in waist-deep water as cold as a Popsicle.

Sputtering, Susan surfaced hands-first and wildly shook her head to clear her eyes of water and hair. The shock of icy water was painful, causing her lungs to desperately haul in extra air. She searched frantically for Griff.

He was standing in the water a dozen feet away. In that instant, his dark brown eyes flicked over her, and transmitted a dozen messages. *You're all right?* He could see that she was. He could see that she was laughing. *The next time you talk me into doing something like this will be a cold day in hell.*

Aaah. His male pride was wounded because he'd misjudged the soft sounds of the rapids from around the bend. Susan started giggling again. Griff surged through the water in pursuit of the canoe. Susan snatched one paddle and one plastic-wrapped sleeping bag, and started towing them toward shore. She was shivering violently by the time she reached the pale, stony shore of a tiny island. And she was still trying to wipe the smile off her face.

She watched Griff for yet another minute. He'd righted the canoe and salvaged the other plastic pack. He looked like a wet, shaggy blond bear with his sleek, silvery head and camel-colored flannel shirt now clinging to his burly shoulders. He was pulling the canoe behind him, very properly subdued... Unlike his wife, his eyes said. His wife—the one with big ideas about shooting the rapids.

She turned away but started to chuckle again as her numbed fingers tried to open the plastic pack containing their sleeping bags. She might not be able to throw a baseball, but she was no stranger to wilderness country, and she knew that this task had to take precedence over changing her clothes: She had to ensure that no water had gotten into their pack. It hadn't. Griff could occasionally be careless about where he dropped his shoes at home, but he was as fussy as an old hen over safety while camping. Their clothes were rolled inside, equally dry, but as cold as her fingers.

Behind her, she heard the canoe scrape over the pebbly bed of the stream as she fumbled to take off her dark, sopping sweat shirt. Goose bumps decorated her skin as cool forest air rushed around her damp flesh. Her tennis shoes felt as heavy as lead, and her toes were miserably squishy; but still she sent Griff a glance dancing with amusement.

"*Why* did I listen to you?" he lamented.

"It was fun and you know it." Her Viking was disgusted with himself; she started chuckling again. She pulled off her shoes and peeled off her jeans; Griff did the same. "It kills me; you can't even hear it now."

"Hear what?"

"Listen," she said softly, and just for an instant they stopped their frantic attempts to get warm and dry.

The roar of rushing rapids was only a murmur now. The forest so totally masked sounds that they might have been in a completely different world. Silence touched their small, private island. Aspens and white birch formed an orange and gold roof; the forest floor was rich, dark earth, carpeted with moss and rustling with dry leaves. Across the winding stream was a jutting finger of land that reflected their own landscape. It was a very old virgin forest, with spaces between the trees large enough to drive through—if a car could make it to this country, an eventuality she hoped no amount of human ingenuity would ever be able to bring about.

Stark naked, they suddenly smiled at each other, anticipating the fire they would build for warmth, anticipating how good the coffee was going to feel in their stomachs... anticipating the night ahead. Each other. The plan had been to find a special spot in the wilderness to camp for the night...

"It'll do," Griff said. His voice came out on a husky note that seemed to echo through the woods.

Crouched on his heels, Griff added another dry branch to the fire. Crackling flames shot orange sparks into the darkness, and a long hiss of smoke trailed off on the breeze. Just ahead of him the stream was jet-black and still, as shiny-dark as the star-peppered sky. Earlier, they'd caught trout and cooked it over the coals, listening to the loons' maniacal cries; before that, Griff had rubbed Susan down until she complained that her skin was neither flint nor steel and she was more than warm enough without his going so far as to set her on fire.

He wasn't convinced. If she caught cold because of that unfortunate dunking, he was going to be furious . . . and from the very beginning he'd made every effort to keep his temper in check for Susan's sake. That she had delighted in shooting the little rapids and was more than ready to take on tomorrow's adventures rather floored him. One minute Susan was so distinctly a lady, all sweet and gentle, all shy and reserved about expressing her feelings, and the next minute . . .

How could he label the other side of her? Still on his haunches, Griff swiveled his head around to study her. They'd lost her hairbrush in the water. A sleeping bag was swaddled around her, her bare toes peeking out from beneath it. Her head was thrown back. The silky mop of dark hair framed a face golden by firelight, sensually lovely in its translucence, strong in its serenity.

The image of a Dakota Indian woman shot through his mind. He wouldn't have said it aloud because he knew she would throw a handful of sand in his direction. The white-man's word, "squaw," had nothing to do with the reality of Indian cultures. The Dakotas were the first Indians to claim these northern woods, their women strong and earthy and fiercely loyal. The nomadic Dakotas often went hungry because of their dependence on the buffalo. It fell to the women to pack up the children and belongings and move with the wandering herds. Their strength was the core of the tribe, the tie that bound the rest together...

Susan was that way. Taking on his troubles by choice, the choice of love. He was increasingly irked at the obsessive way she was taking on his children, however. He'd expected it, because he knew Susan and her capacity for love, but he had not expected that their own relationship would be so quickly shifted by the wayside. The free time he both expected and needed from her seemed to be increasingly spent in projects she created for his children. That Tom hadn't come for the weekend yet seemed only to be another reason to do more for Tiger and Barbara. He wasn't angry with her. But these four days were theirs alone. They'd gobbled up the privacy so eagerly, with talk and sharing and laughter. Perhaps subconsciously he'd wanted to remind Susan that their first commitment was to each other...

And his desire to claim her, his possessiveness, ran deeper in his feelings for Susan than it ever had in his relationship with any other woman; it was as primitive as the landscape around them, as private as the night, as potent as the arousal he felt just looking at her.

"Griff? What are you thinking about?" From the shadows, Susan had been lazily inhaling the forest smells, the pungent earth and leaves, the hint of smoke and sweet crispness of clean air and darkness. Suddenly aware of the silence, she had glanced at her husband and found Griff staring at her, his silver-blond head framing rough-sculpted features, all shadow and taut stillness by firelight. When he stood up, he was a primitive woodsman from a century ago, brawny shoulders barely contained in a rough woolen shirt, jeans molded to long, muscular thighs. His shadow cast a giant's figure on the pebbly streambank, and far into the woods she heard the strange, mournful howl of an animal, primal and hungry.

"Griff?" A shiver touched her. For no reason. Certainly not fear, yet images suddenly crowded her mind when he started stalking toward her, causing her blood to hurry-hurry through her veins as she reacted to the man, to the wilderness at night, perhaps to some primitive instinct that struck a responsive chord in her.

He wanted to make love to her. Now. She saw it in his eyes before his hand so much as touched her... He pushed the sleeping bag back from her shoulders and claimed her hands, pulling her up.

His mouth settled down on hers, with all the luxury of length to length. She rose up on tiptoe, willingly caught in the hunter's snare. He scared the hell out of her when he was like this. It was such damn fun being scared. Danger made her pulse race, quickened her heartbeat. Griff would take, would have, this night, like a warrior coming in from battle, an Indian in from the hunt, a woodsman who had endured months of loneliness. This Griff had a side to his character other than just tenderness and compassion...

One by one, he undid the buttons of her shirt. His palms slid the material off her shoulders. Cold air rushed over her vulnerable flesh... and she suddenly felt terribly sensitive to cold.

He tugged her arms up and wrapped them around his neck, his mouth still hard on hers with a pressure that arched her head back. Over and over, his hands swept the contours of her back, forcing her sensitive breasts against the rough, abrasive wool of his shirt. His tongue stole between her parted lips, probing the inside of her cheek... She was suddenly not so cold.

His hands gradually took a long, slow trail downward, exploring the satin inward curve of her spine, splaying possessively over her bottom, stretching down to stroke the supple muscles of her thighs. His arousal pressed like an announcement between them. *Feel it, Susan.* No games. No soft seduction.

Yet it was a seduction. His thumb and forefinger twisted the button on her jeans; then his hand stole inside, chasing the material down at the same time that he was caressing her hips and thighs. Her underwear was drying on a bush near the fire; he knew that, yet her total nudity seemed to shock him, setting off a flash fire in his eyes as he looked at her. The sound of his ragged breathing set off an answering response in Susan.

She pulled free, just far enough so that she could reach the buttons of his shirt. Her trembling fingers pulled rather than unfastened; she soon tired of the frustration and groped for the waistband of his jeans. Two could play this game. He wasn't wearing anything beneath his clothes either; she wanted to feel flesh, just as he did; she wanted to know this man deep inside her. In her heart, she acknowledged a sudden fierce loneliness she hadn't known was there before, born of the weeks past, of an anxiety over the distance between herself and his children, of a fear that their love had somehow changed as they settled into the real world of being married and living together and dealing with the problems of his offspring.

These days together in the wilderness had destroyed that distance. Griff was a smart, smart man to have insisted on this time alone with her. She had been opposed to the trip; they had so much to do; she hated leaving everything a mess . . . Very smart, her Griff.

When her hands kneaded the tight, taut skin of his buttocks, she heard a guttural groan from deep in his throat and raised her head to look at him. His pupils were dilated, his brown-black eyes all shine and glaze as he kicked off his pants and shrugged out of his shirt. She felt a shimmering, sheer feminine pleasure at the response she drew from him almost without trying . . . and she was more than willing to try.

Her eyes swept up and down, up and down, admiring his muscular body naked in the night, his muscles as sinewed as those of the cougars that haunted the woods, his hair the color of the silver mink, his body as virile and bluntly male as the most predatory of all nature's creatures: man.

He stood still while she studied him; he stood still as she stepped forward again to close that distance and apply the tenderest of silken kisses to his throat. Her fingers skimmed down in deliberate, feather-light attack, sweeping over his arms and shoulders, then his powerful chest, finally teasing more provocatively as a single finger traced the length of all that virility.

"Susan . . ." She heard the guttural warning; his mood wasn't playful. His arms reached for her, but she shivered and danced free of him.

"Shall we play hide-and-seek in the woods at night, Griff?" she whispered. She danced yet another step away, her breasts firm and glowing like satin in the firelight, her supple hips all grace in motion . . . and seduction in invitation. Those clear eyes of hers were full of intoxicating feminine powers, and exulting in them.

In two steps, he had lifted her high in his arms, her soft laughter echoing long into the night. "You think I'd let you walk out there and risk a wolf taking a sweet little nip out of your fanny, do you?" he growled.

"I'm not afraid."

"Aren't you?" he murmured.

The balance of power shifted as he eased her down on the sleeping bag and captured her legs with one of his. His eyes met hers, a dark look of such fierce possession that her breath caught. She was not afraid. Of wolves.

His rough cheek glazed the smooth flesh of breasts already tight with need, already aching for his touch. His whiskered cheek contrasted to the soft texture of his lips, closing first on one breast, then the other, his tongue flicking insistent little messages on her nipples. Her fingers threaded in his hair, splaying in his scalp, encouraging his head that much closer. She was suddenly submissive.

His mouth swept lower, taking in the flat contour of her stomach, hungry for the curve where leg joined torso. Her thigh flexed, of its own volition, wanting to draw him in and hold him, yet she had a terrible feeling he knew her too well. It would happen, but not yet. He wanted to play a very masculine game of let's-see-who's-the-master-at-tease; she wanted to say, Silly, silly, Griff. You can have the title. I never cared . . .

The earth, the stream, the trees, all sent out powerful scents in the night. Susan sent out the faintest, most elusive sweet musk, a fragrance Griff drew in as he breathed, kissing his way down the stretch of her leg, trailing kisses up her side, over the lovely curved hip and waist, under the swell of her breasts.

"Griff..."

He paid no attention, stopping only to smother that whispered cry by touching tongue with tongue. His forefinger traced a leisurely path down her profile—forehead, nose, over those swollen and parted lips, down the vulnerable hollow of her throat to the crevice between her breasts, over her heart, down...

Her whole body shuddered when his finger claimed her moist secrets, his hand cupping that private mount as if laying claim to treasure, inviting the responsive twist of her hips. She whispered something incoherent, almost frantic, and his palm released her. He shifted up again and she thought, *Now. Now,* Griff...

Instead, his lips took that same lazy path, first exploring her gentle profile. Forehead, nose, throat, the hollow between breasts; his lips loved that hollow. He loved the perfect flat slope of her stomach, the soft, curling matt below; he loved her flesh and scent and shape, every mystery that made her Susan. The need to possess, to own, to take, was sheer lust, a full-blooded male instinct that was raging through him, out of control. Nothing could prevent him from possessing her now. Yet the same need to possess, to claim, to take, was just as fiercely a part of love, and he didn't raise his lips again until he had felt a long, low quiver tremble through her entire body.

She was still shuddering when he shifted his hips over hers, when she felt his hand beneath her buttocks, lifting her. That first fierce thrust filled her, caused a thousand stars to explode behind her eyes. She cried out, lost somewhere in a wilderness of consuming passion. So powerful, so painfully intense... She felt her sense of self slipping, her sense of being Susan. The rhythm that locked their bodies together denied that there were two; insisted there was only one.

Her cry of ecstasy matched his, but it was Griff's primal moan that she heard, echoing over and over in the privacy of the night.

8

DUSK WAS FALLING as Griff's station wagon devoured the last miles between Duluth and St. Paul. The goal had been to get home before dark on Sunday, but a side trip had taken them to Griff's four hundred acres, where jack pine was slowly being replaced by aspen and spruce and elm and birch.

"Planting trees in a row will never add up to a woods," Griff had told her. "A forest is a *living* thing. You have to know soil acidity and weather and wildlife... You have to tease the land into trying again."

That was the heritage he wanted for his children, a Minnesota wilderness not so very different from where they'd spent the weekend. Not sawmills, not industrial plants like the ones he owned in St. Paul. Susan leaned back against the headrest, totally and happily exhausted, studying her husband with secret pleasure. He could lash out at business competitors with a machete tongue; very few people saw his idealistic side.

He was dressed in jeans, as she was, and a soft flannel shirt, like hers. Her toes felt sand-gritty, and her hair was tousled, and the very instant she got home she would head for the shower.

In the meantime, she felt perfectly beautiful. Griff's doing.

"Snuggle up and nap," he advised her lazily. "We won't be home for at least another hour."

"I'm not sleepy."

"Those eyelashes weigh two tons and you know it."

Four tons. And all she wanted to do was curl up like a kitten with her cheek on his lap, but she didn't. The long weekend had confirmed too many things, and she wanted to mull them over at leisure. How much she shared Griff's values. How much she loved him.

And Griff loved her. Yes, she had known that before, but somehow in the back of her mind over the last few weeks had come a sneaking sense of insecurity, a nagging suspicion that he'd also married her because he wanted a mother for his children. She thought of the old cliché about the way to a man's heart . . . But that didn't apply to her situation. Griff was a decent cook in his own right; his stomach was adequately taken care of. But his kids were not. And until this weekend, the most horrible anxieties had been creeping up on her. She'd told him nothing of her exchanges with Barbara and nothing of the feelings of inadequacy Tiger dredged up in her. And she wouldn't tell him. Her heart felt full and pleasantly bursting at the moment, and hope was part of that. She would work harder on the kids, in silence. Griff had made it clear that she had her own place in his life and his heart that had nothing to do with his children.

"Too cold?"

"Not really." But Griff switched on the heat in spite of her.

"Take off your shoes," he coaxed.

She bent down to unlace the canvas shoes. "You're extremely dictatorial," she announced sleepily.

A hand hooked itself over her shoulder and tugged her closer until her cheek was resting in the crook of his arm. "I don't want you falling asleep against the door. There's a draft."

"There is no draft, and you can't drive with one hand." Her protest was only a token. They'd had no more than three hours' sleep last night. Then they'd made the canoe trip back to base, rearranged all their gear, and hiked through his forest... Perhaps she was tired. A little.

"Did you know you always argue when you're sleepy?" Griff asked dryly. His fingers sifted gently through her hair, then settled.

"It's my turn to drive. You must be as tired as I am."

"Hmmm."

Her head jerked up, and she stared suspiciously into his eyes, but Griff was suddenly busy driving. "You just turned my own 'hmmm' against me."

"I caught the habit from you. Why bicker when you know you're not going to win? You are *not* going to drive, Susan; you're going to sleep."

She yawned, about to deny it, and then wondered vaguely if she really did quibble over nothing when she was tired. Her cheek snuggled just so against soft camel-colored flannel. It was like trying to find a spot on soft rock; beneath his shirt were muscles that just didn't yield. She couldn't imagine why she was so comfortable.

Her eyes opened instantly, like a doe instinctively reacting to danger. Griff was gently untangling himself from her, but there was something stiff about his movements, a strange, silent tension that had nothing to do with the gentle man whose shoulder she'd fallen asleep on. Outside it was dark; Griff had just pulled into their driveway. His eyes were distracted, black-cold, flickering beyond the car window toward their house.

"What's wrong?" she asked groggily.

"We seem to have company."

"Company?"

He gave her a swift kiss, square on the lips, his eyes holding hers in the dim light of the car for several seconds. "Don't worry, Susan. Everything will be fine."

Worry promptly clawed at her. Griff's expression was grim, his jaw tight and white as he reached behind the seat to start gathering their gear. Susan glanced at the strange white car parked ahead of them. She hadn't noticed it before. The huge elm in the yard threw its giant shadow on the driveway so that it was impossible to identify the person who stepped out of the house, slammed the door, and stalked toward them.

"Where on earth have you been? I've been waiting here more than two hours. For godsake, Griff! At least you always used to have the courtesy to leave me a phone number."

Griff bounded out of the car, slamming his door as Susan fumbled with her shoelaces. Then she frantically reached for the door handle. The grating female voice seemed to flip an instinctive switch inside Susan from *calm* to *nervous*. Hurriedly, she reached up to restore some kind of order to her hair before she stepped out of the car.

Sheila wasn't quite as beautiful as Barbara's photos of her, but the difference wasn't worth mentioning. Her raven-black hair was sleeked back in a coil, aristocratic features were mounted on a spotless complexion. The color of the crepe blouse was indecipherable in the shadows, but the leather jacket had that certain luster, rippling in the darkness when the woman moved; it was unmistakably expensive. And *expensive* was the first label Susan had unconsciously pinned on Griff's former wife.

But not tonight. *Hysterical* was the label tonight. Sheila's hands were whipping around her as she talked, and her venom was clearly directed at Griff. "You care *so much*—so you've always said—but then you turn around and take off without a single thought for any of them. You didn't even leave a *phone* number!"

"Why don't you just tell me what the hell is wrong?" Griff snapped.

"I thought at least there was a *chance* he went somewhere with you; otherwise I would hardly have wasted nearly two hours just sitting here. It would be just like you to scare me half to death."

"Sheila, what the hell are you talking about?"

"*Tom* is what I'm talking about. He's disappeared. Just taken off..."

Griff turned white, a sudden statue in stone. Susan felt a lump too big to swallow form in her throat as she moved swiftly to his side. Sheer anguish fired a terrible bleakness in her husband's eyes as he grappled with the thought of his son gone, missing.

Sheila seemed to see something else in Griff's expression. Her jeweled hands went into overtime, and like a miracle rain, tears started to fall from her eyes. "Griff, don't you dare blame me! After all I do for those kids—*your* kids—they pay me back like this. Barbara won't listen to a word I say; Tiger makes more of a mess in the house than ten normal children. Tom doesn't have a damn thing to be unhappy about. He's got everything. He can come and go when he pleases, he's got a car—"

"Sheila, shut up. This isn't the time to play Lady Macbeth." The statue took life. Griff threw back his head and breathed, and when his eyes focused on Sheila again they were perfectly calm. And as cold as ice. His voice came out in a long, low growl. "What have you done?"

"What do you mean, what have I done? I've worried myself half to death about him, that's what I've done. He went to school on Friday. I went out Friday night. I assume he came home, but he wasn't there when I looked for him on Saturday. He has this girl—"

"You called her?" Griff barked.

"I—"

"Did you call her? Did you call the school, his friends, the police?"

Sheila stared around wildly, spotted Susan and froze. She took in the mop hairstyle, the wrinkled flannel shirt, all of it down to half-tied canvas shoes. Like a dealer in diamonds, she seemed to have an uncanny ability to detect flaws. Susan got the message. "If you hadn't been so busy," Sheila said defensively, "I could have contacted *you*. I can't do everything, you know. You have just as much responsibility to know where your son is—"

Griff muttered something distinctly unprintable and stalked toward the house, snarling at Sheila to follow him, demanding to know where Barbara and Tiger were. If she knew.

"They're at my mother's, of course. *Don't* you talk to me like that, Griff..."

The two faded into the shadows of the doorway. Of their own will, Susan's arms wrapped themselves around her chest. The night had turned incredibly chilly, and her mind was filled with the image of a lonely boy out in that black cold.

Tom was already special to her. She hadn't spent as much time with him as she had with the others, but when he called his father he always made a point of talking with her. Twice now they'd stayed on the phone together over an hour, talking about this and that, sharing a rapport that just seemed to develop naturally. She'd felt the promise of that even during the first dinner they'd had together, and had been sincerely disappointed that so far he'd missed having a weekend alone with them, even though she understood that he had his own interests. There would be other times. She had been so sure that with Tom there would be an easy acceptance, a ready trust she'd believed had already begun...

And now he was missing? Susan felt as if she'd been thrown into nightmare. Instinctively, she felt a dread anxiety about the child who worried Griff most, followed by an unsettling disorientation. Griff had turned into a stranger as soon as he saw his ex-wife. He'd become a cold and furious man barely keeping his violence in check... Sheila seemed to goad him deliberately. Susan tried to dredge up some compassion for Sheila, aware that the woman was frantic with worry, that her panic made her seem shallower and more selfish than she really was. She reminded herself that people weren't themselves in times of trouble... Yet it was Sheila who was in the house with Griff. It was Sheila who was wrangling with him in a way that seemed sadly familiar to them both. Susan had been left outside, forgotten and forlorn, frantic to help but somehow feeling like an intruder.

She grabbed her purse and followed, the weekend of

intimacy fading into the past. The blazing light in the kitchen seemed harsh after the soft darkness; she blinked hard and silently set down her purse. Griff was already on the phone, his face ashen, his movements as tautly controlled as those of an angry cougar. He slammed the phone book down on the table as Sheila nervously paced, lashing out at Griff whenever he gave her the least opportunity.

"I *fail* to understand how you could not know her name—"

"I told you. It's Candice. There was never any reason for me to know her last name."

"You've also all but told me you think he's sleeping with her; I think that's more than adequate reason to know her last name. And God knows how long you've let that go on."

"You've always had the most *archaic* ideas; that's probably exactly why I *didn't* tell you. He's spent the night there plenty of times; that's really why I wasn't even worried at first."

Griff drew in a very long, very slow breath. "You are *not* going to tell me the boy has been out of your sight for days at a time."

"Not for *three* days. That's why I—"

Griff hurled out an expletive, and suddenly there was silence. Sheila slumped in a kitchen chair, staring at her hands while Griff riffled through the phone book and then started dialing.

In those long seconds as the monotonous ringing sound reverberated in his ear, Griff felt an explosion of terror and rage and anguish inside him. Gut terror for his son, rage at Sheila's neglect, and anguish at himself for having failed to snatch his children out of harm's way long before this. From the corner of his eye, he saw the movement of Susan's red flannel shirt and turned.

Susan's face was as white as chalk, and her slim fingers were shaking. She was pouring cream into a pitcher; the coffee was perking, and cups were lined up on the counter. Her fragile profile struck him as incredibly beautiful. She kept moving, all lithe grace and total quiet. Nothing else on earth could have soothed him at that moment. His head was racing out of control with images of his son lying wounded in some alley, in an accident, in trouble . . . yet he kept his eyes riveted on Susan's back, by the time a boy answered the phone, Griff had gained control of his voice.

He pelted the boy with quiet, fast questions. Tom's best friend, John Paul, knew nothing. No, Tom had not been in school on Friday, but then he'd been skipping classes lately. No, nobody really knew much about Candice; she went to a different school, and ever since Tom had started going around with her . . .

Griff knew other names. Steve Baker, another friend. Harley Ross, the principal of the high school. He called one hospital, then another.

Susan placed a cup of coffee in front of him, then quietly set one down for Sheila, who barely looked up. Food seemed the thing then. Not that anyone was going to eat it. But what else was she going to do? Sit across from Sheila and get involved in the cross fire?

"His grades have always been terrific," Sheila snapped defensively. "Why should I get all upset just because he skipped an occasional day at school? It would be different if he were a poor student . . ."

The tirade had lost its momentum. Griff was no longer even looking at his ex-wife. Susan spooned mayonnaise onto slices of bread, aware as Sheila evidently wasn't that Griff was all done shouting. His profile was rigid as he made phone call after phone call, asking the same exacting, probing questions. His fingers mechanically flipped a pencil over and over, tapping first the eraser and then lead against the telephone.

Sheila let out a strangled sound when Griff dialed the police. "For godsake, there's no need for that. It'll be in all the papers—"

Griff held the receiver to his shoulder. "They need to know what he was wearing Friday morning," he said coldly, his eyes like gun metal. At his ex-wife's look of bewilderment, he made a strangled sound of disgust and held the receiver to his ear again. "Probably jeans. We don't know. I do know the make of his car and the license number."

There were no more calls after that. Silence flooded the kitchen like a threatening stranger, and fear touched all of them in very different, lonely ways. Susan knew Griff too well. For a few minutes, he'd been busy making telephone calls. Now he could do nothing but wait. Taking charge came easily to him; sitting helpless was a form of torture.

She placed before him the sandwich that she knew he wouldn't touch, and pressed her palm to his shoulder, letting it linger there. His eyes met hers, just for a second, bleak with anguish, almost unseeing. He covered her hand with his, but his gaze moved past her to his ex-wife again. "You didn't see Tom Friday night; you said you were out. But even if he skipped school, he might have gone back home that night. You must have checked his bed when you did come in."

"Actually, I didn't exactly—" Sheila bit back the rest of the sentence. No one could have missed the way Griff's jaw locked. She stood up jerkily, her dark eyes darting in his direction. "You can have custody of the damn kids," she shot out wildly. "I don't care! I just don't care anymore. You think it's some kind of crime that I need to lead my own life; you always did. It's not as if they're not old enough to spend the night alone on occasion."

As if in slow motion, Griff unbent from his leaning position against the wall by the phone and raked a hand through his hair. His eyes met Susan's again, hers just waiting to pour out a stream of silent communication. *Easy, Griff. She's hysterical, you must see it. Don't say anything that . . .*

He understood. More than she knew, Griff understood. He was well aware that Susan hated the sound of bitter, harsh words. Her fingers were trembling violently, his Susan who always acted out of gentleness and compassion and who loved that in him . . . but Susan had had no experience with women like Sheila.

She was confused and unhappy over his treatment of his ex-wife; he would have liked to offer Susan an apology for that, but he couldn't. What he did do was reach out and very gently smooth back the tousled hair from her cheeks. A chair scraped behind them. Griff's hand didn't falter. His voice was gentle, directed at Susan alone. "I'll be back, honey. Just . . . be here."

"Griff—"

"The police may call back. They'll check the hospitals and runaway centers. Beyond that, there's nothing anyone can do. Susan . . ." He hesitated only a moment. "Stay here."

He didn't give her time to nod her automatic agreement before striding past her into the hall to grab a corduroy jacket.

"Griff? Where are you going?" Sheila demanded, taking a step toward his retreating form. "Didn't you hear what I said?"

Griff strode back into the kitchen only long enough to button his coat, staring impassively at his ex-wife. "I'm going to find my son. And as for what you said about custody, Sheila, you didn't need to bother. You and I both knew already that after tonight the kids were coming here. To stay. With or without the approval of a court of law."

"You wouldn't—"

"I won't need to. Between your questionable morals and your flat-out neglect of our children, there'll be no problem with the courts. It won't take two weeks to hustle this one through the judicial system. I guarantee it."

The door slammed behind him with a little echo.

Sheila stared after him open-mouthed; then her lips pressed together as her eyes darted to Susan. Susan's throat went suddenly dry. Griff was gone . . . Well, she was too perceptive not to understand that he was totally preoccupied with Tom, and that his mind would be working at a thousand rpms. Griff would never sit still and just wait for the police to do his job. He would visit

Tom's friends, go to the places Tom frequented in his free time.

Somehow, though, it was one of those times when she expected him to be superhuman. It was terribly unfair, but she simply did not want to be left alone with Sheila.

Sheila laughed suddenly, a mirthless sound, and turned away to pick up her purse from the floor. "He'll find him. Don't doubt it, honey. The kids *do* come first with him, don't they?" She stood up, smoothing back her hair, her hands nervously fluttering. "When he divorced me—but then I expect you know all about that—I fought like a viper for those kids, and you know why, don't you?" Sheila violently nodded. "You know why."

"Sheila . . ." Susan groped for something to say. "Griff is upset; I know you are, too. If you would feel better staying here, at least until the police call back—"

"I fought for the kids because I still loved him. *Then.* I knew that if the kids stayed with me, I'd still see a lot of Griff. The only thing he ever really wanted from me was to be a mother to those kids. I thought I still needed him then, but I was wrong." She swung toward the door with her head held high. "There are plenty of men around. *Plenty* of them. You're welcome to Griff, honey; you seem like the perfect little mother. You'll have no more problems from me . . . Not that I won't fight for a decent settlement when we hit the courts again. Griff and Sheila and courts are a familiar threesome."

The door slammed a second time. Susan had a curious urge to open the door and slam it a third time, just so she would have her own chance. Sheila had still loved Griff after the divorce. Susan understood Sheila's game. Part of her indifference toward the children had always been a red flag to Griff, a signal that she needed his help. He was hopelessly caught in the complexities of her manipulations, trapped between his love for his children and his unwillingness to promote any involvement with his ex-wife. It was all so complicated . . .

But Sheila had apparently thrown in the towel, finally.

Griff's last threat to his ex-wife echoed in Susan's head. In two weeks, he would have the children... A heated statement in the middle of an argument didn't ensure that he would get custody, but Susan knew from the look on Griff's face that the court system would be wise to work at Griff's speed. She thought fleetingly of how desperately uncertain she'd felt of Griff's love only a few days ago as she had tried to deal with Tiger and Barbara. The weekend with him had dissolved some of her insecurities, but she and Griff had been alone then, with no worries and no tensions. If the children came to live with them, they would rarely be alone anymore. Sheila had said it... Griff's children came first with him.

Her thoughts turned to Tom, a seventeen-year-old boy gone missing, and her heart lurched in anguish. Griff *had* to find him. At this moment, that was the only thing that mattered.

Yet it was two more days before they heard anything more of Tom, a Tuesday Susan was never likely to forget.

9

SUSAN CAREFULLY BALANCED the boxful of books in her arms, aimed a hip in the general direction of her office door, and pushed. The door didn't budge. Blowing a wisp of hair from her face, she tried to readjust the heavy armload of books and turn the doorknob at the same time. One book and then another tumbled from the top of the overstuffed box, and the whole armful tilted wildly when the door opened easily from the other side.

Lanna's wide-eyed stare said it all. "*Don't* ask for help, whatever you do."

"I certainly won't," Susan agreed.

"I'm only the hired help. The assistant you pay to file her nails when we fail to get any big rush of customers on a Tuesday morning." Lanna lifted the heavy box from Susan's arms and headed toward their back stock room. Susan followed, kneading the strain from the small of her back with her knuckles.

"You weigh less than I do," Susan protested.

"So hire us a man. Or let me do the heavy work and lower the rent on my apartment upstairs."

Susan motioned to the shelf where she wanted the box, but Lanna's look said she already knew that. During the next few minutes, they catalogued still more cartons of books, wheeled them back into the shop on a dolly cart, and began to shelve them. The two women exchanged a grin. Two years earlier, Lanna had walked into the store looking for a job; she'd been all of twenty-one, with a bubbly smile and not a goal on earth. At this point, she knew as much about the running of a bookstore as Susan did, and her own shop was clearly pictured in her mind . . . the shop she would have in a year or two. Professional distance hadn't lasted long. Which made it easy for Susan to say, "I was thinking of raising the rent, actually." Her tone was carefully neutral. "I mean since there are two of you up there now, I should get double the rent, right?"

Lanna turned a not totally unattractive pink, in keeping with her flaming hair and freckles. "He's *not* living there. At the moment he just *thinks* he is." She added brightly, "My mother's coming to visit next week."

"That's nice. He's adorable," Susan added, and watched Lanna's pink face turn crimson.

"He is," Lanna agreed. "That's just the problem. Pursue that one, Susan, and I'll probably lose my job by telling my favorite employer to mind her own business."

"Don't risk that," Susan advised.

"So what do you think I should do?" Lanna demanded promptly, and they both chuckled.

"Sow all the oats you want to until your mother arrives," Susan suggested blandly. "Who cares that he doesn't have a job? That he doesn't have any permanent future to offer you? That if he moves in with you, you're the one who will pay the rent and—"

"Thank you," Lanna interrupted. "If you don't mind my saying so, you're worse than my mother."

"I don't mind your saying so."

"Shut up, Susan. I'm enjoying making my Big Mistake."

"Sure you are. He's only been there two nights, and already you're talking about kicking him out."

"I was afraid you'd raise the rent," Lanna said flatly.

"Hmmm." Susan shoved the last book in place. "I won't make you throw him out yet. I'll give him a week, because he *is* particularly adorable. Beyond that, I'll put two bucks on your common sense."

"Only two? Thanks."

"You're welcome."

"I'm certainly glad we had this little talk," Lanna drawled, and strode off deliberately toward the cash register. Susan chuckled, her hand on the dolly cart, ready to roll it back into the stock room. "Hey, boss?"

"You want more friendly advice?" Susan called back disbelievingly.

"I wanted to tell you to stay off the ladder back there. All you have to do is raise my pay, and I'll do all the restocking for the next thirty years."

Susan muttered something indistinguishable. She'd nearly fallen off a ridiculous little stepladder the day before. Dizziness had come over her from out of nowhere. Having a total distaste for hypochondria, she had promptly ignored the incident—or would have, if Lanna had behaved more like an employee and less like a friend. It didn't make sense, anyway. Occasionally, a closed elevator made her swallow hard, but she'd never had a problem with heights.

There had been a little problem getting to sleep lately, though. She and Griff simply hadn't been able to rest. Sunday night he hadn't come in until five in the morning, and had forced himself to go to work on Monday. Then he had spent all of Monday night searching for his son, and today there was still no word from Tom.

Susan's smile faded. She was becoming far more familiar with Sheila's voice over the phone than she had ever expected to. In the meantime, Griff had called his attorney about getting custody of the kids. The phone had been ringing constantly; there had been Tiger and Barbara to soothe . . . Through all of it, Susan was achingly aware that Griff was increasingly terrified for his son, and hiding it well. A lump clogged her throat. She would have done anything on earth to relieve that unbearable anxiety for him . . .

Business picked up around noon. It always did, about the time she and Lanna were trying to snatch a sandwich and had given up on customers in favor of restocking and bookkeeping. Susan was already convinced the store could support a part-time worker in addition to her and Lanna, particularly with Christmas coming. She wanted more time with Griff as well, and the house was a bundle of work. A small sign in the shop window said she was willing to consider applications, but that merely produced a flood of money-hungry students who added to the chaos around noon.

At quarter after one, she closed the door to her office. With a wilted sandwich in her hand, she called Griff. They discussed the weather, her business, his business, and traded anecdotes to make each other smile, all in the space of five minutes; very carefully, they skirted any mention of Tom. If there had been news, obviously Griff would have offered it.

Susan walked out into the shop a few minutes later to find that Lanna had evidently thrown out every customer in the place except one. Lanna never threw out a good-looking male.

The boy was hovering near the door, his hands stuffed in the pockets of his worn-out jeans. His dark eyes were hollowed out with tiredness, which didn't take anything away from his outstanding good looks. With his shock of blond hair, the beautiful eyes, and his clear, strong features, he was a beautiful boy. Brazenly sexual as only a seventeen-year-old male can be, the kind of boy Susan would have run from when she was a teenager. She saw all of that, but did not really think about it. All her attention was focused on those eyes raised to hers, anxious, exhausted, and a terrible mixture of terrifyingly young and all too suddenly old.

Susan stood stock-still for all of a second and a half, praying that he would let her help him. She was beside Tom in seconds, then hesitated, a helpless blur of tears in her eyes. She knew Griff's oldest child so little, and doubted very much that he would let her throw her arms around him. His finger touched her sleeve uncertainly.

"Susan? I was hoping you wouldn't mind if I came to you. Maybe I shouldn't have—"

Reason was tossed by the wayside. She grabbed him and hugged him close. "Thank *God* you're all right." She hugged him again, hard, and finally drew back her hands still on his arms. "We've been so terrified that something awful had happened to you!"

Tom drew in his breath, his dark eyes miserable. "I should have called. Dad's probably furious..."

"Not *probably,*" Susan admitted quietly. "Your mother is equally upset. We'll deal with that later. You look exhausted, honey. Have you eaten?"

He shook his head, but his face had taken on a little color from her full-hearted welcome. "Not since yesterday. I came here... I don't know why. I just had this feeling from the first time I met you that you were someone I could talk to."

"I'm so glad you feel that way." She led him to her office and closed the door. He slumped in a chair as if he were too tired to move again, and Susan couldn't miss the blatant relief on his face when he realized that she was not going to bombard him with furious questions.

In the bottom drawer of her desk, she stashed peanut butter and bread for those days when she couldn't get out for lunch. She made Tom three sandwiches and poured him a cup of coffee. While he was eating, Susan picked up the phone, sending a reassuring smile across the desk when his frantic look telegraphed *Wait, I'm not ready*...

Griff's secretary had to fetch him from a meeting, and his impatient bark into the phone made Susan feel like laughing. "Tom's *here!*" she announced with sheer bubbling pleasure. "He's here at the shop; he's totally exhausted and starving, but he's fine, Griff. After he eats, I'm going to take him home. He belongs in bed or I'd bring him over— What? Of course."

She passed the phone to Griff's son, who hesitated, biting his lip before taking the receiver, looking at Susan fearfully. *Yes, you can, honey*...

Reluctantly, he put the receiver to his ear. "Dad? I—" There was a long silence, but by the time Tom handed the phone back to Susan, more color had returned to his face; there was even the smallest hint of a smile. "He's going to kill me," he informed Susan, but the prospect clearly wasn't as painful as he'd thought it would be.

For what he'd put his father through, he deserved the good tongue lashing that was coming, but it wasn't appropriate for it to come from Susan—thank heavens. Once he was fed, she arranged for Lanna to stay at the shop and close up later, and browbeat Tom into driving home with her rather than following in his own car. It was just as well. The moment his head hit the headrest he was out, one dead-tired pup who couldn't even raise an eyelid.

Susan just looked at him, at every stop sign, every red light, every bottleneck in traffic. That he had come to her in time of trouble touched her, and as she pulled into the driveway and shut off the engine, she studied his sleeping face again, still so white with strain. Every protective instinct she had ever had surged to the surface. She knew why she felt such special sympathy for Tom. This was a younger version of Griff slumped so exhaustedly in the car seat. A young man already determinedly independent, throwing himself violently into life... and foolishly tearing himself apart because he'd made a mistake. No, she didn't know what had made him run off, or where he had been for the past five days. She didn't need to know.

She knew Griff. And suddenly understood why Griff occasionally came home frustrated and angry after having lunch with his son. Two of a kind did not always blend well.

A bit of running interference was in order. For the first time in relation to Griff's children, Susan knew she had something to offer of herself. Finally, she felt that she was part of the family. Griff actually needed her;

Tom actually needed her, and she wanted so very much to be there for both of them.

"I . . . thought she was pregnant," Tom said haltingly, his eyes boring into the Oriental carpet in the living room. "That's what she told me. Like, I'd used . . . protection, Dad, but it's not one hundred percent reliable . . . and when she told me . . ." He hesitated. "It wasn't that hard to get an ID that said I was twenty-one. I bought it for five bucks from one of the kids at school. Candice wanted to get married, and I thought that was what I wanted to do, too. We planned to cross the state line and just . . . and, like no, I couldn't come to you. Or go to Mom. Mom, I never . . . and I knew you'd raise the roof, that you'd find some way to stop me. Too young, no money, no college . . . I knew what you'd say. But all I could think of then was that Candice would be left with a kid, that I'd have wrecked her life, wrecked her chances for going to school . . ."

Griff surged up and out of his chair, his dark eyes aching with hurt as he ran a distracted hand through his hair. "Dammit, Tom," he growled. "I can't believe you didn't know you could come to me with that kind of problem. That you didn't trust me—"

"I've always trusted you. It wasn't like that." Tom jammed his hands in his jeans pockets, stretched out his long legs, and rolled his eyes to the ceiling as if the frustration of trying to communicate with his father was familiar. The gesture angered Griff as well as hurt him; Susan could see it in his eyes, but for the moment she stayed silent. "Look, Dad. I couldn't come to you. It was *my* problem. *My* life that was affected. Not yours. I had to do what was right in *my* eyes . . ."

"You didn't think *our* lives were affected when we didn't know whether you were dead or alive for five days?" Griff snapped.

Tom's eyes went desperately to Susan's, not for the first time that evening. With his hair freshly washed and his clothes hanging on him loosely enough to announce that he had lost several pounds in the last few days, Tom still looked exhausted, half boy, half so clearly man. Susan's heart went out to him. "Just go on," she said gently. "Tell us what happened after that, Tom."

"We didn't get married," Tom said flatly, his eyes following his father's restless movements. Griff could not seem to sit still. Alternately facing his son directly or pacing, he finally leaned back against the fireplace and tried to stay calm. Tom resumed speaking. "I . . . the first night Candy seemed to get ill. And by the next day . . . she wasn't pregnant."

Susan made a small sound of distress. "Lord, she didn't miscarry, Tom?"

"No. Like I guess she wasn't ever pregnant, really. She just wanted to get married, and that was the way she . . ."

"She got her period," Griff interpreted bluntly.

Tom lowered his head. "She tried to pass the cramps off as the flu, and I . . ." He let out a weary sigh and dragged his fingers roughly through his hair in an almost exact imitation of his father. "But she wanted to get married anyway. To some extent, I still felt a responsibility. All the same she *could* have been pregnant, because of me. Everything suddenly got confused in my head . . ."

His eyes met Susan's. "You felt that you'd been taken for a ride by someone you believed you loved," she suggested gently.

Tom looked at her gratefully. "I wanted to do the right thing. Maybe it would have meant I couldn't go to college, but like I'm not stupid, and I'm not lazy; I could have supported her. But I never saw Candy as . . . calculating before. I never imagined she would lie to me about something so important. I thought she *loved* me. I never knew she saw me as a ticket to the right side of town because my last name is Anderson."

Oh, honey, your father knows that story, if only he could see it. Griff and Tom passed the conversational ball back and forth like players in a tennis rally, while Susan sat back, exultant when they scored in communicating with each other, anxious when one of them missed a shot. At least they were trying. Griff loved his son so much, but his natural instincts of love and compassion were shunted aside as guilt told him to play Victorian *paterfamilias*—stern, rigid, authoritarian. And Tom so clearly respected and loved his father, but his pride was involved; he was smarting from having had to come home with his tail between his legs.

Susan leaned back in the tufted wing chair with her legs curled under her, her chin resting in her palm. For a few seconds, her mind blanked out the war. She was exhausted; she'd been through her share of trials earlier. Sheila had been furious that Tom had come to Susan first. To a woman he barely knew. And then *her son* had gone to Griff; Sheila was a poor third. She'd spent an hour late that afternoon closeted with Tom, but she took the time to hurl a few choice words at Susan before slamming out of the house... without Tom. The accusation—that Susan had deliberately and maliciously come between mother and son—had hurt. Badly. From the very beginning, Susan had promised herself she would never do anything to interfere with the relationship between the children and their mother. Of course, there had been more to Sheila's tirade than that. She might as well have used knives instead of words, all of them intended to pierce deeply and twist in the wounds...

Then Griff had come in, exhausted and drained. Normally, he required very little sleep, but three days with almost no rest was beginning to take its toll. His rumpled hair, the circles under his eyes, his tie askew, the deep lines in his forehead...Love for him surged through Susan, coupled with a desperate wish that he would take a less belligerent tack with his son.

Tom would live here from now on, but things were going to be very different for him. Griff expected to know where he was; Tom would not spend his nights with his girl friends; he would stop skipping school...

"Dad. Come *on,*" Tom said defensively. "Like, I messed up. I said I was sorry, and I am. I did a stupid thing, but as for skipping school—you know I got straight A's last semester. I've already got enough credits for college; it's not like I missed anything." He paused, squaring his shoulders, and suddenly looked his father straight in the eye. "And I'm not all that sure I want to go on to college anyway."

"Suddenly you don't want to go to college?" Something had snapped in Griff; Susan could see it and instinctively leaned forward.

"No, I'm not sure I do," Tom said flatly, a belligerent spark in his eyes. "Four more years of school? For what? I can go to work and make some money."

"And just what kind of money do you think you could earn without an education? I swear to God, if I had known about this girl—"

Tom stiffened. "Leave Candice out of it. I—"

"Griff. Tom." Both pairs of blazing eyes shifted unwillingly in her direction. "You're both tired, and I think you've had enough. We can talk some more tomorrow . . ."

"Stay out of this Susan!"

The command was delivered curtly, in a voice both cruel and cold. Susan felt the blood drain from her face as she stared in disbelief at Griff's black-dark eyes. There was no softness of I-take-it-back. He meant it. She felt as if she'd suddenly been relegated to the role of outsider, a third party who mattered not at all at the core of his life. The hurt went swift and deep; she would have preferred a knife wound.

"All right." She stood up, cast a wan smile meant to reassure Tom, and started walking toward the stairs.

"Susan . . ."

She heard Griff, but once she was out of sight she could not take the stairs fast enough.

10

LIKE A ROBOT, Susan turned into the dark hall at the top of the stairs, not bothering to switch on a light. Tears blurred her eyes as she searched out sheets and pillows to make up the bed in Tom's room. The bedroom was still not finished; the rich dark wood and crimson carpeting were masculine and dramatic, choices Susan had felt instinctively Tom would like. Beyond providing a bed, a dresser, and shelves, she'd left the room alone so that Tom could decorate it in his own way. She'd just never imagined that his first night would be quite like this one. When she had made up the bed, she walked soundlessly toward her bedroom.

She slipped out of her sweater and skirt, then lined up her shoes in the closet. Basically neat, tonight Susan was obsessively so, which struck her almost as funny, since she was maneuvering in total darkness. So turn on the light, bright one.

She didn't. She tossed the peach lace bra and slip and her stockings in the hamper, washed her face, brushed her hair. All in the dark. She tugged on a nightgown, pulled down the comforter, and slipped between cold sheets. It was nearly eleven, the luminous dial on the bedside clock informed her. Not an unreasonable time to go to sleep, for a working woman who had to get up at six.

Unfortunately, every muscle in her body was as rigid as iron. She was prepared for a fire alarm or some other emergency, but not at all prepared to relax. Sleep might just happen in the next century.

All he'd said was one simple sentence: *Stay out of this, Susan*. He hadn't sworn at her. Or shouted. It wasn't as if she didn't know Griff was worn out with fatigue and that he'd been harrowed by anxiety for his son. He'd eaten no real food, had too little sleep. And it wasn't as if she didn't know she was ridiculously oversensitive where Griff was concerned.

That was all very well. But Griff had never hurt her before, never shut her out. He loved her in bed; she didn't doubt that. She knew that he loved other things about her, including her ability—and need—to make a home. It had just never occurred to her that he thought she was capable of upholstering a chair but not wise enough to share his problems.

Shut up, Susan. Count sheep, she advised herself. Analyze your life in the morning. It'll still be there. The wound would heal as all heart wounds eventually did. "Men have died from time to time and worms have eaten them, but not from love," as Shakespeare had put it. But for once, book-words offered her no comfort.

So he didn't want her there, not in a crisis that touched them deeply—the first crisis of their married life. She had known from the beginning that there would be problems with the kids; no one had twisted her arm and forced her to put on that wedding ring, and the last thing Griff needed was an oversensitive, overreactive, overemotional female . . .

She had a dozen sheep's wool sweaters knitted by the time Griff hesitated at the door to their darkened room. Susan froze, instantly closing her eyes. He was in his stockinged feet; there was no sound for a few seconds. Then she heard the plop of a linen shirt on the floor, the faint sound of his zipper going down; the rustle of wool sliding down thighs. Then silence.

A cool draft shivered along her spine as the mattress

sank beneath her. Firm, silent hands rearranged the sheet around her, then tucked the comforter meticulously around her neck and breasts and stomach. Not her calves and feet. Griff had discovered the first night they were together that she couldn't sleep with her toes barricaded in covers . . .

A warm thigh slid next to her own, the hard muscle so familiar. An arm slid between hers and her side, and she could smell Griff. Male. Distinctly male Griff. He leaned over her suddenly, slid his arm back out and brushed her hair back from her forehead. She didn't so much as breathe.

"You're hugging that mattress as if it's going to bite you," he whispered. "I'm sorry, Susan."

The tips of his fingers stroked her hair again. "You're so sensitive, Susie. It's one of the things I love about you," he murmured. "I've always had a quick temper. The kids are used to it; a fast explosion and then it's done, but I never meant for you to get caught in the cross fire. For three days, I've had nothing in my head but the image of Tom in an accident, maybe not even alive . . ."

"Oh, Griff, I know that," Susan whispered wrenchingly.

He leaned back wearily against the pillows, drawing her close, his arms wrapped around her as he pressed a kiss on the crown of her head. "When I saw how little authority Sheila's really had over him, something just exploded. I'm sorry if I shut you out, Susan. My anger wasn't really aimed at you. I was angry with *myself,* because I'd failed to keep the kind of contact with Tom that he needed. Of course I want you to be part of his life, part of all the kids' lives. But it wasn't *your* fault that he ran off. It was *mine*. I had to deal with that alone."

"I understand," she said gently, and raised two fingers to his lips. He didn't need to say anything more. She really did understand.

He shifted one more time to settle a kiss on her lips. Soft, gentle, alluring, reassuring . . . She matched his teasing pressure, but when she sensed the almost imperceptible change, a kindling of other emotions intruding in his touch, she pulled back, nestled her cheek on his shoulder, and closed her eyes. "You're desperate for sleep, Griff," she said quietly. "So am I. Everything will look different tomorrow."

His body stiffened just slightly at that subtle rejection. It didn't last; it couldn't. He was too exhausted. He was asleep almost on the next breath, but Susan's eyes remained wide open for a long time. She *did* understand, and she, too, had wanted to make love, to pour balm on that first hurt between them and give it a chance to heal. Yet making love would not solve every problem, and all the questions were still there in Susan's head, questions that refused to go away and seemed increasingly important each day. Would his children ever fully accept her? Was Griff going to accept her help in dealing with them? Would he back her up if she came to a showdown with one of the children?

Susan, this is the perfect time to learn how to relax, she told herself. Now, close your eyes. She did. Susan, let's not make something monumental out of a day that was totally traumatic.

She tried.

It had taken a mere seven days to get a custody hearing, and even then Griff had been impatient at the law's delay. Susan's heels clicked determinedly down the silent hall. On her right stood a row of heavy oak doors. On her left were several tall, oblong windows. At the end of the corridor, she faced a white wall with a single portrait of a judge done in oils. The judge in the picture was named Horshaw. His nose looked as if it had been broken once or twice. Susan turned around.

She began to pace again. On her right this time were the tall, oblong windows; on her left, the huge oak doors. At the other end of the hall were two black and white signs, one marked STAIRS and the other WOMEN. The signs hadn't changed noticeably since her last walk in that direction. She pivoted again.

Horshaw's nose hadn't improved. Actually, he had rather shifty eyes.

She paused at a window and checked on a fingernail to break the monotony. Julie, Griff's sister, had taken Tiger and Barbara and Tom back to their respective schools earlier that morning. The only time Susan had had alone with Griff was the period when the judge talked individually and privately with each child. The kids had been camping out at Julie's apartment for the last few days; the judge had felt that they would suffer less anxiety if they stayed away from both parents until the hearing was over. Julie claimed, all lighthearted banter, that they were having a terrific time. Susan doubted that, fretted over the children's emotional reactions to this whole week of stress, but certainly they had shown no anxiety leaving the judge's chambers.

Nervously, Susan turned again, and at the end of the corridor pushed open the door to the women's room, which she could have described with her eyes closed, should that have become necessary. The pale blue sinks hadn't changed color. The mirror was still spotless. She found one more imaginery wrinkle to smooth out in the peach knit dress that so subtly revealed her distinctly feminine figure. *Not* a maternal choice, she scolded the image in the mirror. Her reflection was tired of hearing the same old thing. She debated using the facilities, but there was really no point. One cup of coffee four hours before had simply failed to produce the need. Not a fifth time.

Pushing the door open again, she headed back to Judge Horshaw. He still looked mean as hell, but he was company. And her stomach was all knotted up. Her mind seemed to have the cognitive capacity of a four-year-old's. One just couldn't tell about Minnesota judges. Not that she'd ever met a judge in her life, but Horshaw's physiognomy was far from reassuring. The issue wasn't Horshaw but the judge on the other side of the oak door, the one with the power to decide whether children belonged with their mother no matter what the circumstances. Sheila claimed she didn't intend to fight Griff for custody, but Susan had her doubts. Sheila was impulsive, unpredictable, and had an ax to grind against both Griff and Susan. Looking at it more charitably, whatever her conduct, Sheila was the children's mother, and what mother wouldn't fight for her kids? A large private settlement in lieu of child support was all she wanted, Griff had told Susan, but she couldn't quite believe that.

Susan had had her own individual interview with the judge, and then had been shunted out of the hearing, just like everyone else. She hadn't even had time to brood about her choice of the peach dress in favor of the nice conservative little navy blue one that made her look bosomy and maternal. The one that she had left in the closet that morning. Now that she was all alone in the hall, she knew what she should have worn, just as she suddenly had brilliant answers for all the judge's questions. Impressive detail, emotional impact, ear-ringing conviction...

But what had she actually said? The children would have a period of adjustment; she'd said she understood that. She had explained her idea of a nurturing home and family life; she'd described the way in which she saw the three children and their individual needs. She didn't know a great deal about children; she'd had to admit that. She would love them, yes. Loving them would not be difficult at all. God, that answer had come from the heart.

What could possibly be taking so long?

The oak door burst open, and she whirled to face it. Griff's gray suit was somber, proper, the maroon tie just so, the starched shirt dauntingly appropriate, blond hair slicked back, neat and conservative... He turned to her, and she caught the dancing dark eyes. Joy, relief, happiness...

Her heels click-clicked, then went into double time. In seconds, she was in Griff's arms; her toes left the floor as he caught her in a bear hug, and suddenly both of them were laughing. Tears in public embarrassed Susan, yet her lashes were shamelessly damp. God, he felt good! How much worry and guilt had he shed in the past few minutes? Tons. She could feel his relief in the relaxed strength of his arms, see it in his dancing eyes, sense it in the kiss he gave her, which a dozen people—including Sheila—made a polite effort to ignore as they walked past.

The children were theirs.

After four chaotic days of moving all the kids' belongings to their house, Griff had announced that he and Susan were going to steal two hours of privacy away from all the confusion. Susan had her choice of restaurants. "I think you deliberately brought me here because you knew you'd be the most beautiful woman in the place," Griff accused.

Susan nodded, pitching into the lobster on her plate with the same enthusiasm Griff was showing. Her eyes flicked absently around the attractive restaurant. Anchors and boating paraphernalia decorated the expensively paneled walls; thick navy carpeting felt lush beneath her stockinged feet. She had tucked her shoes out of sight a second and a half after sitting down. If the kids were only four days new to the household, her feet seemed to have aged a thousand years. The peace and silence of the restaurant seemed appallingly strange.

Four other women were seated at nearby tables. One was chunky, to put it politely. Two were skinny and wore horn-rimmed glasses—a matched pair. And one was a dowager swaddled in brocade. Susan felt definitely beautiful, if a trifle annoyed with herself. It was an evening for champagne, the first evening she and Griff had been alone together to celebrate the last momentous week, but instead of wine, she was sipping water. Her stomach rejected the thought of alcohol; this would have annoyed her even more if Griff had noticed. He hadn't. "If you feel attracted to anyone else in the room, this is probably the only evening in our entire marriage when I will invite you to flirt with another woman," she offered gravely.

"Thank you so much, Susan."

"The one in the purple and red print is probably very friendly," Susan encouraged.

"I'd need a paper bag."

She gulped down a mouthful of water and stared at him. "Was that a vulgar comment?" she asked interestedly.

"Of course not, Susan."

His eyes were full of the very devil; they had been all evening. He stabbed a succulent bit of lobster, dipped it in butter, and raised the fork to her lips. When she'd first met him, such an action would have made her eyes dart around in alarm to make sure that no one was watching. Now she couldn't care less. Griff had been a disgustingly debilitating influence on her sense of propriety and reserve.

He was also the handsomest man in the place. Oh, there was the one self-satisfied number in the corner, all dark hair and brooding bedroom eyes. He'd assessed Susan's figure like a surveyor when she'd walked in. Griff had meticulously seated her out of the man's line of vision, but Susan noted that her husband's eyes occasionally flicked past her, sending out civilized little articles of war. She knew exactly the moment the man left.

The waitress stopped at their table with a pot of coffee. Susan nodded yes. Griff just looked at her. He was having distinct difficulty keeping his hands off his wife. There seemed a special loveliness about her lately, and especially tonight. He'd asked her to wear the peach dress again; that was part of it. So was the special luster to her hair, the sheer joy that radiated from her clear gray eyes. Her happiness bubbled so easily when the people around her were happy, an unselfish quality that stirred protective feelings in Griff. "Susan."

She lifted her head as she wiped her drenched fingers on a napkin, and leaned back, replete.

"Honey, I know you can't feel entirely comfortable with how fast this has all happened with the kids," he said quietly.

"Of course I am, Griff—"

"Three more people in the household so suddenly?" He shook his head, leaning both elbows on the table and pushing his plate out of his way. "If it doesn't bother you, love, it does me. I've come to depend on the private times with you, Susie, and loving the kids doesn't mean we don't have the right to be alone anymore. Naturally, this week has been sheer confusion, but when the tennis racquets and records and whatnot are all in their proper places, it might help if we got someone in to clean the house."

Her eyes widened in alarm. "You mean a housekeeper?"

He nodded. "And someone who'd prepare an occasional meal, be home when the kids arrive from school—"

"Nope." Susan smiled. "Griff, I just hired Jeff to help out at the shop so I can get home by three. That gives me lots of time to take care of the house, and it allows me to be home for the kids after school." She added in a cloaked whisper, "Kindly don't mention it too loud in this feminist day and age, but I happen to like homemaking. Disgusting, I know . . ."

"Honey . . ."

"No one's going to break my china but me. Besides, Sheila will have the kids every second weekend. It'll work out. You'll see." Why she sounded so sure, Susan had no idea. Except that just having acquired a family, she felt possessive about them. No intruders wanted. And surely the incredible chaos of the last few days couldn't last forever?

"I hope you're thinking of the cost, Miss Penny Pincher of the Year, where you yourself are concerned—"

Susan admitted honestly, "The cost is part of it. Why should we pay some stranger to break that first cup? Men never understand about a brand-new set of china. This one happens to be hand-painted."

"It's something like lining cupboards?"

"You're getting smarter with age," Susan said with relief.

Griff chuckled, the darling, and leaned forward to hiss, "Put your shoes on, sassy."

They were leaving? But Griff motioned to the far corner where a handkerchief-sized dance floor was occupied by only one other couple. An ideal chance to get Griff off the subject of hiring a housekeeper, Susan thought fleetingly . . .

Griff's mind was not so easily diverted. Susan was like a mother hen where his chicks were concerned, but having the kids move in was still going to be a major transition for her.

The kids . . . He'd expected a traumatic, emotional week that just hadn't happened, thanks to Susan's gentle takeover and his offspring's intrinsic response to her warmth, even if no one else had taken the time to analyze how very well it *had* gone, despite the chaos of moving. Still, there would be rough spots ahead, and Griff was sorry that the custody hearing was to be followed by two solid weeks of labor negotiations at the plant. And Susan's own work did matter to her, whatever she said. So, if he saw the first sign of stress in her, he intended to bring in outside help right over her stubborn, delectable little body.

Griff led his wife to the dance floor, the pulse in his throat suddenly reminding him of how long it had been since he had held her in his arms. The pianist, uncannily sensitive to his mood, began playing a ballad designed to keep thigh locked to thigh. Her hair smelled like sunshine, next to his cheek. The music seemed to wrap around them both and soothe away all the hectic tension of the last few days.

Gradually, he could feel her body melt closer into his, her small sigh catching his heart. He doubted Susan was even aware of her unconscious tension . . . or its release. For days now, there had been so much to do, so much that needed talking over. They'd both individually taken time with each child, to try to work out any mixed or confused feelings the kids might have over the transition. Susan had taken on Tom until three in the morning one night, with a rapport Griff only wished he had with his son. There had been a great many reasons—not excuses—for crashing into bed and instantly falling asleep, or for going to bed at different times.

For not making love.

Griff was not fooled by all those reasons-not-excuses.

Susan's head slowly lifted from his shoulder, and he found himself looking down into those soft, lustrous eyes of hers. Her lips unconsciously parted, but she said nothing. His thumb grazed the nape of her neck, and her hands slipped around his waist beneath his jacket in response; then she curled close again. "I need you, Susan," he whispered. "I need you more than you know."

He felt that faint tremor of anticipation run through her body, and his lips touched lightly down on the crown of her head, but there was no risking anything else. Not here, not in his present mood. In his present mood, all he wanted to do was make lush, long love to the woman with the sleepy pewter eyes.

He held her closer than a whisper, moving with the seductive rhythm of the love song. It would happen tonight. Susan had been oversensitive to him ever since he'd been a fool enough to snap at her. She'd done a thousand things to convince him she had completely forgotten the incident... except that she'd shied away from real intimacy. Not from lack of love or desire, he knew, but from vulnerability.

And he understood so much more about his elusive wife now; he knew he would try his damndest never again to tread on that vulnerable spot where she was so sensitive. They bickered occasionally. Of course they did. That was part of marriage, and so was unwittingly touching each other's Achilles' heels. He hated hurting her. It made him feel sick inside with a feeling of loss.

"Let's go home," she whispered.

His smile was faint. He paid the waiter and slipped her coat over her shoulders and led her out into a crisp, clear night. She slid into the seat beside him, and once they were out on the highway he lifted his arm and she curled into his shoulder. "I love you," she murmured.

"And I love you, Susan," he whispered back. "So very, very much."

It was a twenty-minute drive home. With a sleepy sigh, she relaxed like a kitten next to him, but when he pulled into the driveway he looked down at her and unconsciously stiffened.

In the shadows, her sooty lashes nestled like lace against her cheeks. Her lips were just slightly parted, one arm curled around his waist. She had experienced so much anxiety in the last few days . . . and her sleep was as deep as a baby's.

Damn, he thought with frustration. He ached to make love to her, and he knew that she had been aching for him, too. *Damn.* Soundlessly, he pocketed the car key and opened the door. *Damn.* Gently and carefully, he lifted her out of the car, whispering something soothing when she started to waken. *Damn.* He cradled her cheek to his shoulder and held her close to the warmth of his body against the night chill, walking slowly toward the house so that his shoes made no jarring sounds on pavement. *Damn, damn, damn.*

11

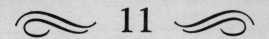

A POLTERGEIST SEEMED to have gotten into Susan's files at the store. Her usual fastidiousness had taken a steep nosedive in the last three weeks since the kids had moved in with them. The roller coaster that hurtled from work to housekeeping to kids kept increasing in speed instead of slowing down after that first hectic week. She seemed to be in control of absolutely nothing. Certainly not the alphabet; M didn't usually follow B. At least it hadn't yesterday.

She was not absolutely sure of anything today, except that the bills *had* to go out this morning. A nagging feeling of anxiety had been dogging her since early that morning, distracting her every time she wanted to concentrate. It was just... Barbara, with that constant list of how her mother did things. And Tiger this morning, the little monkey, had tried to make a spoon go down the disposal, though that at least had proved less chaotic than when he had *somehow* flushed a sock through their plumbing system. He needed some help with his math; at some point today she had to find time to look up a book on that subject; gifted child or not, *why* were they teaching him algebra in fifth grade? She had barely passed it in seventh. And *where was the Bonner file?*

Not in the B's *or* the M's. She was trying so terribly hard to make the transition easier for the kids . . . Disgusted with herself for coming unglued over nothing, Susan whirled in total frustration to see if the Bonner receipt she needed to match the invoice could conceivably still be in the pile on her desk.

The Monet print on the wall suddenly swirled in exploding violet and green. The old corduroy chair, the fig tree that was valiantly trying to grow without a southern exposure, the stack of books in the far corner . . . all of it turned in a fast-swirling kaleidoscope.

Her hands on her stomach, Susan bent forward in her office chair, forced her head between her knees, and willed the feeling to go away. All she could think of was that she'd never fainted in her life and she certainly had no time to pick up the habit now . . .

"Where's Susan?"

There was no missing Julie Anderson's voice, always sassily brusque and bubbling.

"In the office, I think," Lanna responded absently.

Susan forced her head back up as she heard the staccato click of heels approaching. Rapidly pinching her cheeks, she swallowed back the desperate feeling of vertigo.

Her smile was all ready when a bottle of wine clattered down on her desktop along with a package of very good, but very strong cheese. Julie's usual offerings. And just as always, Julie started talking the moment she came even vaguely within hearing range, tossing back her long blond hair and throwing herself into the old green corduroy chair opposite Susan's desk. "Business is absolutely *terrible*. Thank God I got the two of you together; otherwise Griff just might ask me to repay the money he lent me. As it is, what can he do? Without me, you and he would still be sitting on opposite sides of the city. I hope you two are happy, Susan, because I really don't want to show him this month's balance sheets— What on earth are you doing under the desk?" she interrupted herself abruptly. "Did you lose an earring? I swear, ever since I got my ears pierced, I've lost more earrings than I ever did the whole time—"

"Julie," Susan said patiently, "would you remove the cheese?"

"Pardon?"

"Remove," Susan repeated succinctly, "the cheese."

"I thought you liked sharp cheddar— *Susan?* For heaven's sake..." Julie's chair scraped the linoleum as she vaulted out of it. Susan's eyes were closed, her lips were whispering over and over, *"You will not be sick, you will not be sick..."* Julie hastily removed the strong-smelling cheese.

It helped. Susan's stomach had been flip-flop down a deep well, but it suddenly began to lose momentum, and she knew that in just one more minute she would be fine.

"Susan..." Julie's hand touched her shoulder.

Lanna was suddenly standing in the doorway, with a look Susan had seen twice before in the last two weeks. "We'll get you upstairs to my apartment," she said firmly.

"There is *nothing* wrong with me," Susan grumbled. "I didn't eat any breakfast. I've known ever since I was six years old that I feel sick if I don't have breakfast."

"Susan..." Lanna started.

"Should I call a doctor?" Julie asked worriedly.

Susan promptly forced her spine straight, belted her arms tightly around her stomach, and glared at both of them. "All I did was move a little too fast on an empty stomach. Let's not make some kind of federal case out of it."

"We won't," Lanna agreed. "You can just go to lunch with Julie. Immediately." The two women exchanged glances.

"Exactly why I came here in the first place," Julie announced.

Susan stood up then. Her knees felt skittery, but otherwise that green sensation had faded. The thing was, she reminded herself of her aunt. On her mother's side. She'd had frequent exposure to her aunt's hypochondria as a child, and it had caused her to develop an almost phobic loathing for illness.

"You're not going to get a raise for the next eleven years," she told Lanna.

"You gave me two last year. They'll last for a while." Lanna had her coat all ready.

Susan snatched it from her. "I'm *fine*. Please just leave me *alone*."

The waspish tone was so out of character for Susan that both women smiled brilliantly at her. Julie didn't stop the insane kid gloves' treatment until they were seated in a restaurant, eating homemade minestrone and wedges of warm French bread. Susan was keeping up with Julie spoonful for spoonful.

"You really *were* just hungry, weren't you?" Julie conceded finally.

"I told you that."

"You scared the devil out of your assistant."

"Lanna's desperate for someone to mother. She's had the roles all wrong ever since I hired her, but I didn't seem to realize it until the last few weeks." Susan smiled with honest affection, feeling like herself again. "I've got to get her married off. She goes for the stray lambs every time. It wouldn't be so bad if she collected children, but her strays are always over six feet tall with big blue eyes."

Julie chuckled. Lanna's doings always evoked her indulgent amusement. Her smile hovered a moment longer and then faded, and suddenly all her attention was riveted on the spoon in her hand. "I really did come to have lunch with you. To talk about the kids."

"The kids?" Susan echoed in surprise.

"Come on, Susan. I've known my niece and my two nephews a long time. You think the problem wasn't obvious to me when the clan came to dinner at my place last Sunday? My brother never used to be stupid."

Susan, used to Julie's sisterly concern for her, sighed. "Go ahead," she said dryly. "But try to remember that

I'm a big girl, Julie. The kids and I are doing just fine."

Julie's eyes met hers, big, blue, and much more shrewd than her wine-and-cheese-shop profits would lead one to suspect. "They're eating you up, Susan. *Why* haven't you told Griff? Surely you know what Sheila's like. She gave them nothing, so naturally, they saw you coming and held out their hands. It's called *taking advantage,* darling." She said the last two words very clearly, as if to emphasize the message to her sister-in-law.

Susan sighed and leaned back, absently regarding the busy comings and goings of the lunch crowd in the cheerful little restaurant. "Whether you can understand it or not, I happen to have a bad case of attachment to those three. I sometimes have a mad urge to glue little signs on their foreheads: MINE. And they're not really giving me a hard time, Julie, not nearly as bad as I expected. Oh, Barbara sometimes goes a little too far. That I'll admit. But then, she's going through a period when she needs to test me."

"As in every time Griff's back is turned," Julie interjected demurely. "She learned those tricks from a master; you *must* realize *that.*"

"Don't," Susan scolded bluntly. "Do you think this has been easy for Barbara? She must feel as if she's turning her back on her mother to come and live with us—and Sheila isn't an ogre, you know. I'm not her judge, and neither are you."

"Don't *you* forget that the judge didn't just look into my brother's winsome eyes and suddenly decide to give him custody; he talked plenty to those kids and to their mother. Don't waste your time feeling sorry for Sheila, Susan. Maybe this is her chance to get her life together. Finally. At any rate, those kids weren't forced to live with you; they had their say. They must care for you. And as far as I'm concerned, that means you should have the right to slam them against a wall occasionally when they get really out of line."

"You've always had this terrible problem expressing

yourself," Susan said with mock compassion. "You never speak your own mind, never come out and say what you're thinking."

Julie burst out laughing. *"You're* the one who got me started—at least on this subject. Telling me about that book."

"What book?"

"Tough Love. Wasn't that the title? Something about kids testing you because they want you to set limits on their behavior, because it's a natural human need to establish rules. Well, if that's true, then you've got the right to say *no* to them, Susan. That won't stop them from loving you."

"So wise," Susan marveled. "Remind me of this conversation if we ever get you married off and you have your own children, will you?" Susan gathered up her purse and coat and snatched the bill from the table. "I've got to get back. I've got a thousand things to do this afternoon..."

Julie stood up reluctantly, casting Susan a rueful look as they made their way to the front of the restaurant. "Tell Griff the kids are bugging you," she murmured as they walked outside.

"You were a perfect darling to invite me to lunch," Susan said warmly. "Normally, I would have holed up in the back room with peanut butter and stale bread."

"Tell Griff," Julie repeated ominously.

"This has been a perfectly delightful conversation," Susan assured her.

Julie didn't usually admit that some mountains are just too high to climb, but this time she gave up on her sister-in-law, threw up her arms in defeat, and climbed into her car.

Susan found a shopful of customers when she walked in the door, and had no time during the busy afternoon to mull over Julie's lecture. Griff had been busy as hell the last three weeks; he couldn't possibly see what was going on between her and the kids. If he *did* see, he seemed happy with the chaotic transition from honeymooners to a family of five. And essentially, the kids seemed just as happy. None of the arguments and resentments she had worried about had materialized.

She was the only one floundering. Was she the right kind of stepmother for them? She was not usurping Sheila's role, not coming on too strong, not pushing any closeness before the kids wanted it...Oh, Tough Love had sounded good in principle. But Barbara seemed to need a full-time chauffeur, demanding that Susan drop whatever she was doing on the instant; yes, Susan could get tough and request a little consideration. She knew Barbara was using every excuse to test her, but that didn't change Susan's feeling that Barbara was having the hardest time in the transition and needed love and understanding. She would soon tire of a one-sided battle ...wouldn't she?

Tiger and the football that broke her grandmother's vase...Susan *could* have yelled. It would be easy to yell at Tiger as she followed the urchin from room to room, picking up disasters, along with socks, shoes, school bags, and crumbled cookies. But his own mother had never forced a single rule on him, and suddenly Susan was supposed to step in and play the heavy? The psychologists said it was all right to yell, as long as you directed your anger at the behavior rather than at the child—but would a divorce-torn ten-year-old really make the distinction? It probably hadn't been all that long since Sheila had read him Grimm's fairy tales, with all those wicked stepmothers...

And Tom...she'd made the mistake of telling him that he should feel free to play the stereo. A mature seventeen-year-old would be into jazz, or maybe even classical music, right? Wrong! Try hard rock, at ear-splitting volume from the moment she walked in the door until dinnertime...and after dinner until Lord knew when. Of *course* she could tell him to turn it down. That wasn't even a minor deal, but it *was* rather a major one that they were getting along so well. Three strikes and you're out, remember? At least Tom was her success story. But that wasn't really the issue. It was all the thousands of things at once, so sudden, so overwhelming . . .

Tell Griff, Julie had insisted. But tell him what? That she was less and less sure where she stood with her husband, how he expected her to deal with his kids, what he valued in her as a woman? A bedmate? A mother? But the role of wife seemed to be steadily sinking in a morass of confusing adjustments. Griff was becoming the stranger across the crowded room, but the song had a lot less romance when the crowd was made up of children.

On top of everything else, a flu bug seemed to have been chasing her for the last few weeks. No, it hadn't caught up yet, and Susan had no intention of falling ill. She'd beat the damn thing with vitamin C and sheer willpower, because the thought of even trying to cope with Griff's kids if she weren't healthy . . .

Which you are, she insisted to herself. Healthy as a horse. Strong as a mule.

Vulnerable as a buttercup. Oh, shut up, Susan.

Susan stretched as she got out of the car and shook herself. She'd been on her feet most of the afternoon, and the kinks had settled in the most unreasonable muscles—like where she thought she hadn't any. She gathered her purse and raincoat and started toward the house, wincing the moment she opened the door.

Pop music *was* music wasn't it? Actually, it might be. It wasn't the kids' fault that her father had raised her on Debussy. The album cover for this particular record showed two half-naked men who shaved their heads and wore pancake makeup, and at this point, she thought she deserved the Medal of Honor for being able to identify the record jacket that went with the raucous sounds coming from the living room.

She glanced into the kitchen and unconsciously winced again at the sight of the dirty dishes scattered around the counters in a long trail that spilled over onto the table. Unbuttoning her coat with one hand, she picked up the milk with the other to return it to the refrigerator before it spoiled. Then she put the little heap of cookies back in the cookie jar and replaced the cover. Filling up the sink with soapy water, she rapidly gathered glasses. Three children. Eleven glasses. That kind of mathematics seemed to come with teenagers. Oh, yes, she understood all about the adolescent herding instinct... At least, come ten o'clock, she'd know where her children were—not to mention an assortment of other people's children.

When she opened the closet door to hang up her coat, her arms automatically reached out for the avalanche of jackets that cascaded down on her. Hangers were boring. If one shoved one's jacket in the closet and rapidly closed the door, obviously no one would know. After neatly hanging up the jackets, Susan hurried into the bathroom to run a brush through her hair and wash her hands; then she reached out for a towel.

There wasn't one, of course. *Why* did she persist in expecting to find one? Obviously, you used a towel only once, and then you tossed it down the chute. Fastidious personal cleanliness, filthy personal habits: That whole scene seemed to come with teenagers, too. At first, Susan had been rather bewildered by the mound of towels that seemed to mysteriously mate and multiply by the washing machine. She was learning.

Vigorously shaking her hands to dry them, she dared to venture closer to the living room in spite of the music assaulting her eardrums. Four lithe bodies were stretched out on the carpet, with Barbara, center stage, making up the fifth. Susan saw no purpose at all in entering the room, other than to pass through and use the excuse to touch Barbara lightly on the shoulder en route. A hello kiss was not yet appropriate, but every once in a rare while Susan got the impression Barbara was waiting for her to walk in.

Books littered the carpet; so did record albums, shoes, assorted jackets, and of course, more glasses.

Susan assured herself that she would have plenty of time to clean it all up before Griff came home. She had an hour and a half left. Way back when, she didn't know how much she could accomplish in ninety minutes, but she was becoming a master of fifty-two pick-up. And the point was that Barbara should feel free to have her friends over. The point was *not* a little extra housekeeping. She'd told Griff she liked homemaking, right?

She poked her head into Griff's study, to see Tom folded up with a book. He lifted his head long enough to utter, "Hi, Mom-Two," before lowering his eyes again.

"Everything go okay at school?"

"Par."

"Where's Tiger?"

"Upstairs."

Tom could be very talkative, when he wasn't concentrating. His boots weren't going to mar Griff's desk, because they were rubber-soled, she reminded herself. After throwing a "Home, Tiger!" up the stairs, she rushed back to the kitchen to finish the dishes. She paused in the middle of that task to hurry downstairs and toss a load of towels into the machine.

Before she could take the first step upstairs to change her clothes, she paused, suddenly frantically remembering that she hadn't taken a thing out of the freezer to thaw for dinner. Dinners for five refused to appear out of nowhere. With just Griff, it had been different. On a rough day, they had simply gone out, or Griff had brought home Chinese delicacies; otherwise, they had simply put their feet up for a while and later fixed something together over wine. Now that she left the shop at three o'clock—usually—she'd made a point of telling Griff he no longer needed to help. Griff liked to cook, but it seemed far more important that he spend his free time with the kids, and he'd been working such long hours lately . . .

"Susan?"

Tiger's face appeared at the top of the stairs, and her face relaxed. "Hi, sweetie."

He was all excited, all big eyes and laughter. "I've got the neatest thing to show you."

She followed him, laughing at his bouncing impatience. Dinner would have to wait. "Come *on,*" he insisted. "Hurry up!" At times like this, when he was so eager to share, broken cookies and even broken heirloom vases were mere bagatelles.

Up the stairs, past Tom's room—Lord what a mess—past Barbara's, which surpassed any destruction a bomb could cause, and finally into Tiger's. Toys as well as school clothes littered the floor, but Susan reminded herself that there was still plenty of time to get it all back in place before Griff came home.

"You're just not going to believe this," Tiger informed her.

She didn't. The hamster cage had been relocated from the basement to Tiger's room the day Tiger moved in. The project had not worked out quite as Susan had expected. She was the one who cleaned the cage four times a week and fed the animal that happily bit her each time. She had anticipated *shared* responsibility . . . but no, she hadn't pushed it, because not a single rule had been imposed on Tiger in Sheila's house. In time, she kept thinking. This extra work, like all the rest, was largely her own doing . . . Susan understood that, but something inside her refused to admit that in trying to make the kids happy and easy and comfortable she had dragged herself into a pit she couldn't get out of. Children needed consistency, and she'd consistently indulged them, so . . . There must be a fallacy there, but who had time to analyze?

Crouched down next to Tiger, she stared in horror at the hamster cage. The one little animal had turned into seven. The six smaller creatures were tiny and hairless and ugly.

"I thought you had to have a boy and a girl to have babies," Tiger speculated.

"I did, too," Susan replied dryly.

"Isn't it neat?"

Susan had loved animals from the day she was born, but all she could think of was the seven bites she would get from now on, every time she put her hand in the cage. "Neat," she agreed, hoping it sounded convincing.

"I've been watching the whole thing. But I still don't get it. I thought you had to have a father *and* a mother. How could she have the babies without a father?"

"Hmmm." Not an impressive answer. Susan rallied. "If we'd bought the animal from a pet store, this probably wouldn't have happened," she explained. "But I got this hamster from an ex-friend. There must have been a father and mother together at one time."

Tiger wrinkled his nose. "What do you mean—*ex*-friend?"

"That's very involved," Susan said vaguely. No wonder Beth Smith had been frantic to find a home for the damn hamster! She rocked back on her heels. The smell from the cage threatened to overwhelm her, and she had cleaned it the night before.

"We'll have to have more cages," Tiger said in a rare burst of practicality.

More cages to clean. Susan closed her eyes wearily, but then opened them, her eyes suddenly soft on their youngest child. How many women would have killed for such an endearing kid? Suddenly, Susan was overpowered by a sense of blessing. "Pretty special, watching them being born?" she questioned.

Tiger nodded, still speaking in whispers. "I was even scared to breathe." Those beautiful eyes darkened. "I told Barbie to turn down the stereo because I was afraid the noise would be upsetting to a new mother. Barbie said the whole idea of hamster babies was stupid."

Susan grabbed his shoulder and drew him close, kissing the top of his head. He had such sweet-smelling hair, her boy, all boy. "It isn't in any way stupid," she reassured him, meaning it. For a short moment, she even felt reassured herself, in a completely different way. There were times all the turmoil was completely worth it. She recalled suddenly the Sunday morning all five of them had been at the breakfast table, and Tiger had gotten a fit of the giggles that infected all of them; the time Tom had talked with her until three of the morning, about politics and feelings and perfect worlds; the times Tiger snatched up a hug out of nowhere; the times even Barbara ventured out of her hostility to just girl-talk; the night Griff had taken them to McDonald's and somehow forgotten his wallet and she and the kids had dredged up every last penny they had, even Tiger . . . well. This moment to be cherished was with Tiger, and she wouldn't have cared if he'd dragged her out of bed at three in the morning to see his hamsters being born.

"I really think we better change her name from Archibald," Tiger whispered.

"I think we'd better," Susan agreed.

The music from below suddenly stopped. Susan's ears felt as if they'd been offered a reprieve from torture. Stretched out in front of the cage, whispering with Tiger, she never heard the footsteps in the hall, only belatedly saw Griff suddenly appear in the doorway—after Tiger whirled and bounded to his feet. "Hey, Dad! Come see this!"

Griff strode in, crouched down between them and peered obediently into the cage, commenting with all the appropriate hushed enthusiasm that was required of him. His manner was calm and easy, as it almost always was with the kids. Only Susan, so sensitive to Griff's moods, felt the undercurrent of tension emanating from him.

"You're home early," she remarked, delighted he had not had another late night of labor negotiations. Perhaps that delight was what had eclipsed all consciousness of what he must have seen on his way from the front door to Tiger's room, she would speculate later.

"I'm home early," he agreed. His eyes met hers for the first time, and held. He was furious. She didn't need it spelled out.

He vaulted to his feet in one lithe movement, snatching Susan's hand to bring her to a standing position whether she particularly wanted to get up that minute or no. "You'll watch your charges for a few minutes while I have a word with Susan, won't you, Tiger?" He asked lazily.

"Sure!" Tiger's eyes were riveted on the cage; he didn't even look up.

Five fingers forced their way between hers; Griff's without question being the stronger and larger. She didn't mind being hustled into their room. The door closed between them and chaos with a distinct snap.

12

GRIFF RELEASED SUSAN'S hand. His suit jacket hung open; his hands were hooked on his hips and one leg thrown forward. "Are you going to tell me how the hell long that *circus* has been going on?" he demanded furiously.

"Griff. I . . ." If her pulse weren't beating so fast in her throat, she could probably think. Anger radiated from him, and yes, her man had an occasional burst of temper . . . She had just never expected it to be directed toward her. "If you're talking about the house . . ." she started uncertainly, now recalling the sight that would have greeted him on his journey to Tiger's room. "It would normally have been cleaned up by the time you got home. You're early, Griff, for heaven's sake. I just got home myself."

He knew that. And for two seconds, Griff debated between shaking her and putting her to bed. He didn't give a hoot in hell about the chaos in the house. It was the exhausted circles under her eyes that tugged at his heart. He had suddenly deduced that she'd applied fresh makeup to cover them before he came home every night during these last weeks. Preoccupied with labor negotiations, he'd never dreamed he was coming home to smiles that had been freshly manufactured for his benefit. Now he saw her without the lipstick smile, without the smoothing over of circles and fatigue lines. And the sight of Susan, exhausted and anxious, cut him to the quick. "What the *hell* do you think you're doing?" he growled.

"Griff..."

"It's a damn good thing I *am* early for once," he snapped. He loved her, now more than ever, but it was for her own good. "We're going to get a few things straight here, and very quickly, Susan."

He stalked out of the room before she could say anything further. She heard him barking for Tiger, then striding down the hall and taking the stairs like a general. Not a general. A Viking, because Griff was not quite as civilized as a military man with a machine gun in his hand in the middle of a war.

Tiger shot out of his bedroom, casting a startled glance in her direction before vaulting down the stairs two at a time. She heard *"Barbara!"* and a moment later *"Tom!"* Then there were doors closing, silence, and more doors slamming. She stood in the doorway to their bedroom, her arms clasped under her chest, her mind not really at all sure what was going on...and not absolutely sure she wanted to know.

By the time Griff stalked up the stairs again, there was total silence below. His shoulders filled the space in the hall as he strode toward her, his brown eyes still like kindling on fire. His voice rivaled thunder. "They're gone," he spat out. "Tom will take charge for at least two hours. He's leading the parade to McDonald's—the one next to the video-game arcade. Which is neither here nor there. You and I are going to talk. Right now."

"I—"

"And first, you are going to *sit down and relax,* Susan. Dammit," he added distractedly. "How the hell long has this—*sit down*. We're going to cover the subject of kids once and for all."

He stopped raging the instant he realized how white her face was. He took his temper for granted, having grown up in a family of volatile personalities; with four children and two adults shouting had been the only way to get heard. Only . . . Susan heard in whispers—he'd forgotten that. And she was standing in front of him like a fragile nymph with huge eyes, sick with anxiety. "Susie . . ."

She took a breath, her first since he'd reappeared. "Griff, we all need time. It's not an easy transition for the children, and I've only been trying—"

"I know *exactly* what you've been trying to do," he fired back. He'd handle his brood. He loved them, but if they didn't know a nugget of gold when they saw one, they had a swift lesson coming. Only a fool could fail to see how precious Susan was. Well, he might raise monsters, but he had no intention of raising fools. But his concern wasn't just for the kids. He couldn't bear to see Susan, a full rose in the sun, shrinking back to the tightly closed bud she had been when he'd first met her. Hiding her feelings, keeping them walled up tight . . .

Confused and upset, Susan stood perfectly still as Griff took a step toward her. He blamed her for being unable to control the children; she knew that. And she was guilty; there was nothing to say. Except, Griff, would you please stop looking like a volcano about to erupt? I can handle ninety-seven loads of wash a week, but I can't handle your anger.

Yet . . . for a furious man, his fingers, when they undid the first button of her blouse, were exquisitely gentle. "You're going to put on a robe. And get your feet up." The dictatorial growl was again contradicted by his gentle fingers on the second button. And the third.

Griff pulled her blouse out of the waistband of her skirt. She stared up at him bewildered as he untangled the gold chain at her neck, letting the delicate necklace fall into the hollow between her breasts before slipping the blouse from her shoulders. He had very dark eyes, her Griff, radiating a thousand vibrant emotions. Anger was not the only one, suddenly.

"Griff . . ."

"You're going to get some rest. You're exhausted. I'll go down to the kitchen and make us some sandwiches, and then we're going to talk, Susan."

He glared at her, as if waiting for opposition. She wasn't about to argue with his master plan; she was just rather startled by it. The last she knew, Griff was furious; now he was talking sandwiches. And then he wasn't . . . talking. It took several seconds for him to locate the button of her skirt. Most of her skirts buttoned on the side; this one buttoned in back. He pushed her head to his chest as he unfastened the garment. The blue wool skirt slid soundlessly to the floor and lay there in a rumpled heap. It cost an arm and a leg to have the cleaners press wool skirts; Griff didn't seem to care. Not about the proper care of wool skirts, not about children, not about the debris downstairs, not about anger.

She was still trying to grapple with his change of mood when his hands hesitated, resting on her hips over her cream-colored slip. Those hands suddenly turned caressing, slowly moving up to her ribs and over her lace-trimmed bra to the hollow of her throat. As his thumbs teased her chin up, his movements were all slow motion.

Looking at him, she felt a shiver creep along her skin, raising her sensitivity to his touch. Damn, she felt vulnerable. He was still fully dressed in a suit, her massive Norwegian man with his dark, searing eyes.

It had been a very long time since they'd made love. She didn't know why the thought struck her, when it was so obvious that neither of them was in the mood. Griff was furious, and she was miserable . . . and other emotions seemed to have come from absolutely nowhere. He peeled off his suit jacket, his eyes never leaving hers. He tossed it on a chair; his shirt followed, then his belt. The pile of clothes on the floor kept growing.

And the silence in the room continued to drum in her ears, a silence that hadn't been part of the house since the kids had come to live with them. Dusk was settling like a velvet stillness from the west windows; night was coming, that *feeling* of night enfolding her as he reached for her.

She felt swallowed up, so fast. His big, cool hands enveloped her, and the first kiss on her mouth arched her neck back. So hungry, all warm and hungry . . . Her hands reached up around his neck, instinctively soothing, her touch tentative and careful; she wasn't absolutely sure where Griff was coming from. Every inch of her skin knew the desire to be held, to be wanted as only Griff had ever wanted her; her mind refused to go quite that fast. A half-hour before there had been hamsters and a terrible headache and all that noise and the look on Griff's face when he had confronted her with it all . . .

"Let it go," he whispered. "Let it be, Susan."

He made it sound so easy. He made it seem so easy. His knuckle grazed the swell of her breasts as his fingers released the front hook of her bra. Her breasts were free, aching for the touch of his cupped hands. Her soft flesh was oversensitive, made painfully tender by the sweet, fierce messages Griff kneaded into it.

He lifted her up and settled her on the bed, folding the spread impatiently out of the way. Then he knelt, peeling off the silk half-slip, peeling off the sheer hose, peeling off the small wisp of silk panties. He looked at her, savoring the golden sheen of flesh with a possessiveness that sent a blind rush of lush sensations through Susan's bloodstream.

She would have reached for him then, all willing, but he barely gave her the chance. With a low, guttural groan, he stretched out over her, raising her arms above her head like a pirate pinning down his captive. He loosened his hold then, but not before she'd enjoyed the sensation of hand to hand, breast to breast, thigh to thigh. That closeness had been a message: They were one person, not two. Griff knew her well; he would know all of her, claim all of her; there would be no holding back.

His lips crushed her and then began to travel. The rough-smooth sensations of his soft mouth and bristly cheek sent a thousand erotic calls echoing through Susan's head. Griff was making a valiant effort at patience. He was in no mood for slow, sweet lovemaking. His mood was a fierce, urgent desire to consume. His lips swept over her flesh, from her hard-tipped nipples to the tiny curve of her stomach to the softness of her thigh; the tempo of his breathing increased, and hunger vibrated through him like a shudder.

She slid her hand down over his hip, then let it turn inward, knowing exactly what she was doing to him. Both of her hands moved to his head when he loomed over her; her fingers tightened in his hair, pulling him down, so that a kiss blended exquisitely with his silken smooth thrust into her body. Her spine arched for him, legs twisting. She knew the rhythm, the fierce, primal rhythm . . . The climb started from her womanly core, a fever as heated as his, a desperate need that tumbled not only her defensive walls but the whole world. Just Griff. There was only Griff in that place . . .

Yet from somewhere other emotions intruded, desperately unwanted. Tension from the real world, fear, anxieties not resolved . . . The feelings surfaced, not as conscious thought but as a faltering in intensity, a slip in rhythm for Susan, something she couldn't help . . . But she could pretend for Griff's sake. It didn't matter. Griff did; loving him was what counted, and when she felt his body grow taut in a last effort to control his pleasure for her, she urged him on, whispering, her body arching into his, her hands ceaselessly encouraging him.

When his body exploded in release, she felt a special joy that came from the heart rather than from the sensual pleasures of the body. She stroked him, curling up next to him, listening to his heartbeat gradually slow, loving the sheen of moisture on his body and the sheer exhilaration of the feel of him next to her,

It was several minutes before he shifted, before he slid down next to her and turned. His lips touched her forehead; his hand cradled her head as he lifted her face to his. "It was good for you?" he whispered.

"Very good," she whispered back, meaning it. It had been good—if not in quite the way he meant.

He sighed, his eyes very dark over her, very grave and almost menacing. Still, a faint, seemingly amused smile touched his lips. "I had no idea exactly how much we needed to get straight in this relationship," he scolded, his voice still husky and low. "Don't do that to me again, Susan. Ever."

"Do?" She was bewildered.

"Fib." He shook his head, scoldingly, his displeasure reinforced by the delicate nip he took at a spot directly between her neck and shoulder. "I was faster than a speeding bullet. I'm not denying that. As you are on occasion. Maybe I was just in a hell-bent hurry to break down your defenses before we even tried to talk, because I could see you repairing old walls, love. Anyway, the reason doesn't matter. But you fake nothing with me, Susan, you understand?"

The kiss that landed on her mouth was rough and sweet and very, very clear. "We take care of each other," he murmured. "Don't ever, ever think again that I'm not willing to take care of you."

His hands slipped down with caresses, all silk, tantalizing and gently alluring. Giving her back the mood she'd thought was lost, driving away her quick-quick fear that the children would come back too soon, disallowing, this time, all conscious and unconscious hesitation. His lips followed his hands, and he was so intent on ingraining a particular lesson of love that he didn't let her go until she had shuddered violently in her own ecstatic release, once, twice, three times.

Susan went through the evening in an oddly sleepy, desultory haze. At some point, she remembered munching on a sandwich while she let Tiger slaughter her in a game of checkers, and at another point she remembered curling up next to Griff on the living room couch as all five of them watched a half-hour sitcom that was perfectly dreadful . . . but they all laughed. Only later did it occur to her that she and Griff hadn't had the talk Griff had insisted they have when he came home like a storming Viking.

That occurred to her about the same time that she wandered in the kitchen to find the dishes done. Moments later, she walked upstairs to find that the kids' bedrooms had been miraculously tidied up. Good fairies? No, obviously more potent forces were at work. There were fresh towels in the bathroom.

She was too tired by then to think it out. Tucked in next to Griff with the comforter pulled up to their chins, she felt her eyes drooping with fatigue. It was Griff who had used a very silent, very heavy hand with the kids behind the scenes; she knew that.

She couldn't help feeling that Griff must be disappointed in the way she was handling his children. One tongue lashing from him and his brood jumped, but she just wasn't built that way.

A nameless fear was beginning to haunt her nights—that in other ways she wasn't built as Griff must have thought initially. They'd had to snatch those moments of lovemaking; was that how it was to be? Granted, this was a period of transition, and yes, she loved the children. She also valued privacy. She needed it and had needed it all her life. She needed privacy with Griff as well. Their own relationship was still new . . . too new, she thought fleetingly. Loving him, she was afraid to admit that he just might be disappointed in his choice of a wife. She had not been blessed with either self-sufficiency or confidence. And she wanted—needed—more of Griff than a quick, stolen moment now and then.

When Susan woke up, the place next to her in the bed was empty, and she had a strange, queasy feeling in her stomach. Those sandwiches for dinner had obviously not agreed with her, she thought wryly, and dragged herself sleepily out of bed. The clock showed six o'clock, but

Griff was already up and out. She knew that, because today was Friday, and with any luck the labor negotiations at the plant would end today.

Yawning, she snatched up bra and pants and slip. By the time she'd showered and put on underclothes, it was twenty minutes later, and she rapped on the three children's doors to waken them. *Why* was her stomach playing leapfrog? Ignore it, she advised herself. Pulling on a yellow crocheted dress, she ran a brush through her hair, applied a minimum of makeup, and gave up her bathroom to the morning lineup. Not that there weren't other bathrooms, but even Barbara now demanded that she be allowed to feed the fish.

Downstairs, Susan switched on the kitchen light and began to do the dozen assorted chores it took to start the day. Pack the lunches; prepare some breakfast; take something out of the freezer for dinner; remind Tiger where he left his book bag; throw in a load of laundry... Every precious second of that morning hour counted, and, of course, this morning a few were lost. The downhill slide started when she poured herself a quick cup of coffee, tried to take a sip, and felt her nostrils flare at the revolting smell.

She set the cup down. Waffles for Tiger; Tom liked two eggs sunny-side up; Barbara would have to be coaxed into eating one slice of toast; she was afraid of losing her sylphlike figure; nutrition was "stupid." While she cracked the eggs, Tiger's head suddenly showed around the door, his hair slicked down with water, his face most definitely grave this morning.

"Susan," he said seriously, "I think we're going to have to have a cat."

"We are, are we? Honey, I think I saw your gym sneakers under the couch. Your book bag's behind your coat."

"We need one," Tiger continued. "We've always needed a cat. Our whole lives, this family has never had a cat."

"You're tired of the hamsters already?"

Tiger shook his head, perching directly next to her on the counter so that she had to reach around him. "The hamsters are neat, especially the babies. But they really smell. Cats don't smell."

Susan's stomach did not want to be reminded of the hamsters' odor. She poured batter into the waffle iron, fielded Tom's kiss on the cheek, and responded to his affectionate "Morning, Mom-Two" while handing him his plate of eggs. Then she headed toward the refrigerator to make a cheese sandwich for Barbara's lunch. A cheese sandwich was calorically acceptable to Barbara; nutrition was still "stupid." The girl had fallen asleep last night with *Thirty Ways to Develop Your Bust* clutched in her hand; apparently, eating balanced meals wasn't one of the thirty ways.

Barbara came into the kitchen yawning. The uniform it took her nearly an hour to get into consisted of jeans and a clinging sweater—mohair this morning. Her hair was brushed back simply. Her eyelashes looked suspiciously dark and velvety, but that was one of the few battles Susan had subtly won about a week before. The tiniest touch of Vaseline accomplished the same thing as mascara, and Griff didn't threaten to disown her because of Vaseline. Barbara, on a rare day, could see reason.

"Morning, Susan."

"Morning, honey." She served Barbara's toast and Tiger's waffles, along with three large glasses of milk—Tiger's was chocolate—then rapidly took away Tom's empty plate and opened a fresh package of cheese for Barbara's sandwich, keeping one eye on the sink to be sure Barbara didn't try to pour her milk down the drain.

Smoked cheddar. She'd always loved it. Yet when she opened the package, Susan stepped back, feeling waves of nausea engulf her. She took a deep breath, and then a second. "Barbara," she asked idly, "do you think you could make your own sandwich while I throw in a wash?"

All three kids suddenly looked at her. Barbara got up from the table, rubbing her hands together to brush off the last of the toast crumbs. "Sure. We wouldn't want to overtax you, Susan. I got the drift last night." Her look was bitter and her tone sarcastic.

Susan swallowed. "If your father said something to you," she started quietly.

Barbara laughed.

"Shove it," Tom suggested to his sister.

Barbara clammed up, and began to slap cheese slices between pieces of bread, not looking at Susan.

"Honey, I only asked you to help with the sandwiches because—"

"Like it's perfectly all right. I got the message," Barbara snapped.

Tom pushed back his chair, glaring at his sister in disgust. Tiger looked from brother to sister, wide-eyed. "Susan," he said finally, "did you forget we were talking about getting a cat?"

13

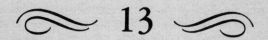

An hour after the kids had left for school, Susan walked into the store, past Lanna, past the stacks of books and crafts, and into her office, where she promptly closed the door. Five minutes later, she emerged and motioned to Lanna at the cash register. "We're going to have to close for a few minutes," she said absently.

"Fine." Nothing threw Lanna.

"I need you to drive me somewhere," Susan said.

"Fine." Lanna grabbed her coat. "Your car or mine?"

"Yours."

Susan turned the Closed sign around, walked to the parking lot in silence, and gave directions as Lanna started the engine. Lanna's face carried a smug, relieved look, which no amount of careful lip-biting could hide.

"Look. I'm *not* ill," Susan informed her irritably. "All I'm going to do is spend thirty dollars to find out that I'm not only *not* ill, but that I seem to be turning into some kind of hypochondriac."

"You are as far from being a hypochondriac as anyone I've ever met in my life. Look, Susan, you haven't missed a day of work in four years except for vacations. In my particular scheme of things, I call that kind of virtue an illness."

"So cynical," Susan said wryly.

"Realistic."

"I just hope there's a pillow under you when you *really*

fall, because I have this terrible feeling you're going to fall hard."

"You came to work this morning looking green," Lanna commented pleasantly, always eager to steer the subject away from herself.

And Susan felt green. She was damned tired of feeling green. Once the kids were off to school, she'd felt suddenly so dizzy she could barely stand, and being alone in the house had oddly frightened her. So had driving alone to work. She was worried about Griff, and Barbara had hurt her, and what she had finally told herself was that she needed to . . . cope better. That seemed to be all it amounted to. And how could anyone cope well whose stomach was turning somersaults on a regular basis?

"Did you tell your husband?" Lanna questioned as they pulled into the parking lot of the doctor's office.

Susan ignored her. Obviously, she wasn't about to burden Griff with a bunch of hypochondriac nonsense. For that matter, she thoroughly resented wasting money on a physical examination. T-shirts for Tiger, jewelry for Barbara, popcorn for a year for the teenagers who devoured junk food at all hours of the day and night . . . "Just go back to work," she told Lanna.

"I'll wait for you."

"You will not wait for me. You will return to the shop and reopen it. I'll take a taxi back later."

Lanna shifted too fast in response, chugging the car out of the parking lot like a bouncing Jeep. Susan would have smiled if she hadn't been entering the doctor's office. The place smelled of alcohol and disinfectant; the walls were white, with an occasional framed print that jarred with violent color. Susan remembered the magazines from the one time she had had bronchitis; undoubtedly, they still carried those latent germs.

The nurse ushered her into the examining room, all serenity and efficiency.

"I'm really perfectly all right," Susan told her.

"I was just looking at your chart. It's been ages since

you've had a complete physical."

"I don't need a *complete* physical." The nurse stuck a thermometer in her mouth, then took it out and examined it before resterilizing it. She took Susan's blood pressure, and then made a sound in her throat that Susan couldn't interpret. Such dramatics. One could be dying and this nurse would never say so.

"Please take off all your clothes now, Mrs. Anderson . . ."

Which was one of the reasons Susan hated to go to the doctor. Nudity and Griff went together. Nudity and cool examining rooms and strangers simply didn't, and she had the terrible feeling she was going to feel the same way when she was ninety. And Dr. Grey was worse than a stranger. He had delivered her some twenty-eight years before, and had taken far too much for granted ever since.

"Hi, honey," he began, and went downhill from there.

"I'm perfectly healthy," she told him.

He nodded, all gray hair and endlessly patient smiles. "You sounded terrified on the phone. You say you've had a number of dizzy spells?"

"No one has dizzy spells nowadays. There is nothing wrong with me. I skipped breakfast one day. And lately maybe I've been a little tired . . ."

"Lie down, Susan." His soft blue eyes peered at her over his spectacles, when the first part of the examination was over. "You can relax any time."

The last of reasons why she hated doctors. Relax—the most popular of orders. She closed her eyes, waiting for pain that never happened, wishing that Griff were with her and at the same time extremely happy that he was not, and feeling miserably sick to her stomach. Dr. Grey redraped the sheet over her less than five minutes later, and his kindly eyes viewed her with a rueful expression.

"About seven months to go, sweetie. I hope to heaven your husband wants to be present for the delivery, because you're going to make one hell of a patient."

The drugstore was across the street. Vitamins for this, supplements for that. The dizziness and nausea . . . even Dr. Grey had nothing for that; evidently it just occasionally affected some pregnant women. It would undoubtedly pass in another couple of weeks.

Pregnant.

Griff's baby.

"There wasn't the least thing wrong with me," she told Lanna later, and worked with a daunting speed until closing time. Like a buried burst of energy in her system, elation would suddenly surge forth out of nowhere. She kissed Mr. Riverton when he came in with the mail; she hugged Mrs. Bartholomew for doing a proper stitch on her crocheting. She ate a peanut butter sandwich for lunch and then forgot and later ate another peanut butter sandwich.

It was really a terrible shock, pregnancy. It shouldn't have happened so soon, her mind warned her. If at all. Griff had his children; they had never really discussed having their own . . . Oh, they'd touched on the subject, but only casually. He loved kids and knew the maternal itch was catching up with her before they even married; but the subject had never been a source of worry. If the providence that had brought about their marriage wanted to bless them with children . . .

But not now.

She couldn't even cope with three now, much less four. Yet that feeling of elation kept coming over her, like a miraculous secret that stole her heart away every time she thought about it.

"You're all right?" Lanna questioned her once.

Susan looked up from the shelves, startled. "Of course I'm all right."

"Susan," Lanna said patiently, "you were humming 'The Battle Hymn of the Republic' at the back of the store. Now that most of the customers are gone, if you want to go home . . ."

Barbara would be disgusted when she heard the news. Tiger would undoubtedly be interested on the same level he was for his hamsters. Tom . . . Tom might not mind.

And Griff? The one who really counted . . .

How stupid she was! The last thing on her mind these last two months had been her period, nor was she a calendar-follower, so perhaps she could forgive herself for not having paid attention there. But birth control . . . There'd been no need to consider that issue in years, certainly not on the night she met Griff. After that night, though, he had promptly brought up the subject, bluntly, Griff-style, fully prepared to take on the responsibility and totally comfortable discussing the options. She had delicately implied, Susan-style, that she preferred to take care of the problem herself.

Seeing as she was so responsible, there should have been no problem. What she hadn't known was that it would be extremely difficult to prepare for a man who could ignite with desire while reading the Sunday paper and drinking his morning coffee. Particularly since he kindled the same firecracker impulses in her. Unfortunately, she could clearly remember the first night they'd christened the house. The very last thing on her mind . . .

Or were those all mere excuses? From the very beginning, she'd wanted his baby.

But not now. She just couldn't handle any more children right now.

Susan wiped her hands on a dish towel, glanced absently around the kitchen to make sure that everything had been put away, and switched off the light over the kitchen table. Leaves were plastering themselves against the windows; it was dark outside, and a storm was howling through the night. In a rage to bring in winter, she thought idly, as she cupped her hands between her forehead and the window to look outside.

All the beautifully painted fall leaves were gone; the tempest was roaring, and the huge elm looked like a shiny black ghost in the rain. Susan unconsciously shivered, and just as unconsciously put a protective hand to her stomach. She stepped back from the cold draft and walked toward the bathroom to run a brush through her hair.

She was one of those weird creatures who loved winter, but not on a night like this. The baby troubled her, and the atmosphere of impending storm seemed to have intensified her concern. One moment she was elated and dying to tell Griff; the next moment she felt unsure and frankly pessimistic, both about Griff's reaction to the news and about her own ability to cope with his kids, plus another child on the way.

The clear gray eyes that ususally looked back at her from the mirror were distinctly cloudy tonight. Her hair refused to behave for the hairbrush, another minor annoyance. Griff liked it when her rag-doll mop decided of its own will to curl and wave; she didn't, and never felt her best when her hair was unruly. But then, Susan, she chided herself, ever since you've been pregnant, you've been making mountains out of molehills. She turned away from the mirror after straightening the cherry-red sweater and patting it down over her jeans. She felt utterly despondent.

Nothing had gone right from the minute she'd walked in the door. The house had been silent, and she'd reveled in the serenity for a minute or so. It was a Friday night, and Tiger had been given permission to spend the evening with a new friend three doors down from them. Barbara had left to spend the night and the following day shopping with her mother and grandmother. There had been no blaring stereo and no endless chatter and no clutter to pick up. It had seemed like heaven. But for some insane reason, she missed all of the confusion, and paced restlessly until Griff and Tom came home.

Griff had burst into the house in a mood of high elation. His labor negotiations were finally done, after two long, grueling weeks. He felt a strong loyalty toward his workers and was determined to treat them fairly and even generously; the negotiations had gone well, but he was still hyper; the adrenaline hadn't stopped pumping overtime yet. He and Tom had managed to clash on the issue of Tom's seeing "that girl" again before either had even gotten around to changing their clothes.

Griff had won the argument because he was in that sort of mood—take charge and don't back down—but the atmosphere at the dinner table had been far from trucelike, and Susan had felt her inner wires tighten to the breaking point. Now, as she walked through the silent kitchen and hall, pausing before entering the library, she could hear that Griff and Tom were at it again.

Griff had started a fire and closed the drapes against the gloom of the storm. He'd changed into jeans and a flannel shirt, but he was still projecting the aura of a businessman, command and authority radiating from his strong profile. A wave of love touched her, partly because he was a beautiful man, partly because she loved the way the firelight limned austerity on his features, partly because she knew and respected that dominating side of Griff so well . . . and because she knew there was another side to him that was not that way at all.

Tom was slouched among the big fat cushions of the couch. His long, jeaned legs were stretched out, his ankles crossed, his body as relaxed as his face was taut with impatience.

"Tom, I want you to go to college," Griff said flatly, his voice low and careful, so careful that Susan knew he was wary of failing at communication with his son. "Your grades are outstanding, as we both know. It would be different if you were suited to some kind of trade. I've got no snob thing about college, but I think it would be the best choice for *you*. Your *own* abilities—"

"Dad," Tom said wearily, "you want me to go into business with you. I've known that since I was knee-high. What you really have in mind is that I get a degree in marketing, or accounting, or economics."

"That's your choice. You'll pursue *your* own interests."

"Oh, yeah. Sure." Tom leaned back, staring for a moment at the ceiling as Susan slipped into the room, curling up in a chair near Griff with her legs tucked under her. "But *my* interest is history, Dad, not business. I want to teach, not manage—anyone or anybody. What you do is fine, but it's not for me. I'd have told you this a long time ago, but I knew you'd only get upset."

"I'm not upset." Griff, so clearly upset, leaned forward as he ran a hand through his hair distractedly.

This was the first time Tom had ever mentioned his interest in history, and Susan's heart went out to Griff. Her husband worked because he loved to, and succeeded because he was that kind of man; yet Susan knew in her heart that part of that momentum was the thought of building a business he could pass on to his kids someday. And even Tom's runaway episode hadn't changed the dreams that Griff had for his older son. Griff recognized Tom's quick brain and independent nature and ability to get along with people—barring, unfortunately, his own father.

"If you have some misconceptions about the kind of work I've done all these years," Griff started slowly.

"No, Dad."

"I've never taken a penny dishonestly. And if you think there's no excitement in the business world, Tom, you're mistaken. We face a different challenge every day. We've built an outstanding reputation over the years—"

"*You* have, Dad." Tom added quietly. "Maybe Tiger will be interested in the business, or even Barbara, but not me."

Griff fell silent. Susan could see the pulse working in his throat, the throb of his Adam's apple that was so purely male. Tom was the classic younger version of his father, but with defiance taking the place of Griff's strength, as it so often does in the young. His eyes unhappily trailed his father's every movement, but his jaw remained rigid.

"Of all the subjects you've studied in high school," Griff reasoned finally, you've done best in math, drafting, science—"

"So I'm a whiz kid," Tom replied, an attempt at humor

that failed. He threw up his hands. "That stuff comes easy; I'm not saying it doesn't. History never did, and I had the most terrible teachers . . . that's the point. A good teacher . . ."

"You can pursue history as a pastime," Griff growled.

Tom turned away. "Dad, I am *not* going to major in business."

"Well, you're sure as hell not going to major in *history*. Do you know what a history teacher earns in a year?"

But he would not reach Tom by talking about salaries. Susan knew that. Whatever career Tom ended up in, at this point in his life he was desperate to make a mark that said Tom-not-Griff. Griff was hurt and uncomprehending. Neither Anderson had the patience of a stone, and Susan stood up, afraid that their talk would deteriorate into harsh words from which neither one could back down. "The point is that he will at least go to college. That's good enough for now, isn't it, Griff?" she said quietly.

Tom's eyes darted in her direction, desperately grateful. Griff went totally still.

"Students have to take required courses during their freshman year," Susan continued hesitantly. "A little bit of everything. There'll be plenty of time for him to choose a major later on."

"I'm not going to change my mind, though," Tom said flatly.

No, darling? You changed your mind very quickly over Candice once you ran into certain realities, and you might just run into realities again with other decisions, but I'm certainly not going to press that. "I wasn't suggesting you should change your mind," Susan told him, with perfect honesty. "I was only suggesting that college is still the best of all possible places to test out your interests—and abilities."

Tom hesitated. "As long as I can take history courses . . ."

Susan suddenly couldn't look at Griff, because she

couldn't think of a single occasion when he would appreciate anyone speaking for him. "Your dad has no objection to your taking all the history courses you want," she told Tom. "And if you end up really wanting to major in history, there'll be no problem, Tom. But it won't kill you to take a few business courses as well, just to acquire a practical education. Then maybe you can work with Griff in the summers to earn some extra money and to find out what the business world is like. In the long run, you can do whatever you want to, whatever makes you happy. Your dad and I both care deeply for your happiness."

Tom went up to his room a short time after that, and Susan was left with a very silent Griff, crouched in front of the fire with his back turned to her.

"You're angry with me for interfering," she suggested quietly.

"No."

But he didn't turn to face her. "You are," she insisted. "Griff..."

He turned then, rising from his crouched position. His body was as taut as a wire; his brooding eyes held hers. "Susan, from the first, Tom's had a special feeling for you. I'm glad of that; you've been there when he needed you...and I'm not angry. I could see what you were trying to do—give him time, in the hope that he'll come around if he's allowed to do so without losing face. Dammit, I agree completely with you. All I really want is for him to be happy, though I admit I'd prefer for him to at least take a shot at the business before he just rejects it out of hand. But you even covered that base..."

He turned away again, opening the draperies to stare out the window into the stormy night. "The thing is, every time I try to have a conversation with him, I seem to fail abysmally. Everything you said was right, Susan...but I just never seem to bridge that communication gap with him myself. I was determined that tonight we'd get past those walls, maybe even get angry at each other, but all the same keep going until we got somewhere together . . ." He looked back at her, not insensitive to the distress in her eyes. "Honey, it'll happen another time. I'm not blaming you. Now, if you don't mind, I think I'll go walk off some stress. The weather," he added wryly, "is perfect for it."

Susan sat absolutely still until she heard the front door close, her stricken eyes staring unseeing into the fire. She'd hurt him—inadvertently, but she'd hurt him. Not seeing that he desperately needed to thrash this problem out with Tom, she had jumped in to smooth the troubled waters on one of those occasions when she really didn't belong, when no one belonged but Griff and his son.

He'd hurt her once with hastily spoken harsh words; she'd had no idea then how much more terrible it would be to know she had hurt him.

She was tired and overwrought and afraid that she was failing in this marriage, and she didn't really feel well. She thought of the baby, and burst into tears.

14

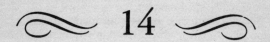

SUSAN COULDN'T REMEMBER the last time she'd walked in the rain. The leather boots reached almost to her knees, and her raincoat was buttoned up to her throat; she wore gloves and a vinyl hat she'd bought on a whim a long time ago. Not an inch of her was wet, though the rain kept pouring down, splashing on the pavement and forming puddles.

It was four o'clock in the morning, a strange time to take a walk. No one was out on the streets, neither cars nor passersby; no windows were lit up, and the heels of her boots made sharp click-clocks on the pavement of the quiet St. Paul streets.

Why she had gotten up in the middle of the night and stolen from Griff's side she didn't know. She had left a brief note on the kitchen table in case he woke and worried because she was out of the house, but she could no longer remember what it said.

She had to get out from under, that was all. One minute everything seemed to be all right. She adored Griff; she loved his kids; she desperately wanted his baby; she was safe and secure in a job and a home she loved. Only a fool would expect more.

The next minute she knew she could never become the mother Griff needed for his children. A baby would only add to the reigning chaos. She knew Barbara would never accept her; she hated the hamsters; one more blaring rock band would drive her completely over the edge . . . and she couldn't bear to disappoint Griff, to let him know how swiftly she had been totally snowed under. There was no peace and no privacy in their marriage, and there never would be. A few stolen minutes with Griff now and then would not give them a chance to build a really solid marriage.

Susan's head was roiling with murky thoughts; she came to no conclusions. She didn't want to go home right now, that was all. Coward, she told herself sadly, and found herself facing the small book store with its sign, THE UNICORN, in a cheerful little window with a small light. She walked around to the back, the dark alley blocking out some of the ceaseless wind and rain, then ascended a small flight of wooden stairs and knocked quietly, then louder.

Lanna finally opened the door, clutching her robe to her throat, her blue eyes sleepy and her red hair in a disheveled halo around her head. Her mouth dropped open when she saw Susan.

"You shouldn't open your door to anyone in the middle of the night," Susan told her.

"Come in," Lanna said, and all but pulled her inside, ignoring the spray of raindrops that sprinkled on her as she took Susan's coat. "What on earth are you doing in the middle of the—"

"I seem to have run away from home," Susan said absently. Was *that* what she was doing? Her fingers touched her temples, massaging the soft skin, as if she were rubbing away a headache she really didn't have.

"When I ran away from home as a kid I always carried peanut butter and jelly sandwiches and a teddy bear," Lanna remarked, watching her worriedly.

Susan dug her hands into her pockets. "I don't seem to be that well prepared," she admitted. "I was hoping you'd put up your landlady for the rest of the night."

"Sit down, shut up, and I'll get you some tea."

Lanna disappeared into the kitchen, and Susan sat

down and looked around distractedly. She suddenly thought of something. "If you have someone here..."

"Contrary to what you like to believe," Lanna called back, "I really don't have overnight guests all that often. Naturally, men queue up outside my door, just waiting for the opportunity. After all, I'm not only smart and beautiful, but also extremely creative." Lanna's head whipped around the door frame. "I told you to lie down."

"You told me to *sit* down," Susan corrected. The apartment was small, but charming. Lanna's favorite color was pale yellow, an unusual color for a couch, and canary, orange, and bright blue pillows abounded on it, leaving little room to sit. Bookshelves reached the ceiling, and candles stood in rainbow-colored groups; beyond the living room was a kitchen, then a bedroom and one other small room of indefinable use. Lanna sewed, so that must be her workroom.

"Here." Lanna set a mug of steaming tea on the table in front of her, along with a napkin. "Now, what shall we talk about?" she inquired brightly. "Macramé? South America?"

Susan picked up the hot mug and promptly set it down again. Her hands were trembling. The hot liquid splashed on her fingers, and she suddenly swallowed, very hard. Something was stuck in her throat that swallowing failed to dislodge. Something thick and aching...

"I'm sorry. God, I'm sorry. I didn't mean to sound— I just wanted to make you smile." Lanna leaned over and hugged her hard. "You've always been an angel to work for, you know that? I love you like a sister, Susan. The teasing you put up with about my pretending to mother you— But you've always been the one to come through for me—the job and the apartment and a large dose of common sense when there was no one else to give me a swift kick in the butt. Whatever it is, you know damn well I'll help you..."

"I just..." Lanna moved away, and Susan lowered her eyes, rapidly blinking away tears, her voice coming out increasingly shaky. "I just... lately I just can't seem to handle anything well. It's . . . expectations. Expectations I had of myself, expectations Griff has of me . . ." Suddenly, she felt exhaustion flood through her as if she were a wind-up toy that had finally wound down. She threw back her head and folded her arms around her stomach. "The cheese incident this morning with Barbara, and the mess I made with Tom tonight. Griff doesn't have time for me, but what the hell am I, a child? One minute I feel like a slave, and the next minute I feel so selfish. And when Griff and I *do* have some time alone, I'm so tired . . ."

"I understand," Lanna said gently. She studied Susan for a long moment and then informed her, "I'm putting you to bed."

Susan shook her head. "I didn't mean to inconvenience you. I just thought that if I could lie down on your couch until it's time for the store to open up . . ."

"Hmmm," Lanna commented, a trick she'd picked up from someone she was inordinately fond of. "You found out from the doctor that you were pregnant, didn't you?"

"Yes." For one short instant, Susan managed a wan smile. "I *told* you I wasn't sick."

"I guessed a long time ago. About the day you started shelving the fiction on the nonfiction shelves." Lanna chattered until she had Susan safely tucked in bed, her jeans and red angora sweater replaced by a borrowed nightgown. "We're not exactly of a size, but tomorrow you can borrow one of my sweaters . . ."

The suggestion fell on deaf ears. Susan was gone, her head nestled on the pillow and her eyes closed in exhaustion. Lanna pulled the bedcovers up to her chin and left the room, closing the door behind her.

She didn't awaken until past ten, and then to a completely silent apartment and a lukewarm sun peering down at her through the long, narrow window of the bedroom. For a moment, Susan was disoriented and lay still, staring in sleepy confusion at the ceiling.

Twenty minutes later, she opened the door to her shop

below, wearing a pale yellow sweater of Lanna's that was a tad too small, and the jeans she'd worn the night before. She'd helped herself to toast and a quick cup of coffee, but there was no time for more than that. Regardless of what a mess she had made of her life, she had a responsibility to her business, which she had no intention of foisting off on Lanna. And in that frantic rush downstairs, she had realized that no clear-cut answers had appeared from thin air, that she was no more prepared to face her fears than she'd been the night before.

Lanna spotted her over the heads of six customers. She bit her lip, then was forced to direct her attention to the people who were bombarding her with questions. Saturday mornings were like that. Susan forced a cheerful smile and dug in, taking over as she had once been very, very good at taking over. It could only last so long, though, the forced brightness. As soon as the customers thinned out, she headed for the shelves. She had a good excuse to fuss over the shelves, of course. Saturday morning people picked up a thousand books and always put them back in the wrong spots; keeping order in this chaotic atmosphere was an endless job, but truthfully, she liked it. She liked the people, and she liked the work, and she liked the feel and smell of books . . . and this morning every single thing she did brought on an unexpected threat of tears.

She was on her knees, working on the bottom shelf in the back, when she saw a worn pair of tennis shoes next to her. The wearer was shifting his weight, first to one foot, then to the other. Her eyes rose slowly, to jeans with patched knees on skinny little legs, to a brand-new sweat shirt emblazoned with the slogan, "Put a Tiger in your tank," to a pair of big brown eyes she knew very well.

"Like where were you this morning?" Tiger asked. He crouched down, delighted to have finally caught eye-to-eye attention, and offered her an effortless grin. "I've made my own breakfast lots of times, you know. I like to make my own breakfast. But not this morning, Susan. This morning I had all this stuff to tell you . . ."

His look was faintly reproachful. It tore every single string in her heart. "Tiger," she started unhappily.

"Tom's coming to get me in a minute," Tiger informed her. "We're going to Aunt Julie's."

"That's nice."

"I think we should go to McDonald's tonight, don't you?"

"I . . . don't know," Susan said, and had to look away from those big brown eyes. She put two more books on the shelf and took down three others.

"You want me to help you?"

"No, darling." Lanna must be responsible for the apparition of Tiger. Susan was going to fire her . . . after injecting her with slow poison.

"Susie?" A tentative imitation of his father.

She was forced to look up into those limpid eyes.

"We can work out a deal," Tiger suggested happily. "I'll get rid of the hamsters." He hesitated, having gotten no immediate response. "Like that's the deal. Okay? If those hamsters bother you—"

God in heaven, she was going to burst out crying. This wasn't Lanna's doing. It couldn't be. This was Griff's kind of dirty pool. "There is no reason in hell for you to get rid of your hamsters," she choked out to Tiger.

"You shouldn't say hell," he told her, disturbed.

"I know that, darling."

"So why did you say it?" he inquired interestedly.

"I haven't the slightest idea."

"There must be some reason."

"Grown-ups can occasionally be idiots."

He concurred with a nod of his head. "And if you want me to pick up my room, Susan . . ."

She jerked up to a standing position, only to face another pair of dark eyes. "Tiger's going out to Aunt Julie's car," Tom said bluntly. "I want to talk to you."

"*I* was talking to Susan," Tiger informed him resentfully. "Just because you're bigger . . ."

"Aunt Julie says she's going to take you for an ice-cream cone."

Tiger reached over to Susan, expecting a good-bye hug and some understanding as to life's priorities. He got both. That firm, skinny little body was already wriggling impatiently, but she could hardly fail to get his message. Love offered, gift-wrapped at no extra cost.

Tom was intrigued with her office, poking into corners, opening the files, testing the corduroy chair, leaping up again. "What's this?" He motioned to the typed list on top of her desk.

"That's the list of the week's best-sellers," she answered.

"And is that supposed to mean they're actually good books? Recommended reading?"

"Best-sellers are the books people are buying the most of. And yes, sometimes they're the best of what's come out—sometimes, but not always. If you don't read much, it's not a bad list to go by . . ."

Susan could have gone on. She was being shredded apart inside, and it would have been much easier to talk books, but Tom sliced through that, very casually. "You're the best thing that ever happened to my dad."

"I . . ."

He straddled a straight chair, undoubtedly intent on looking manly. Susan settled back behind her desk, grateful for the support of her desk chair.

"Mom fed us a bunch of junk about Dad after they got divorced," he told her flatly. "How he didn't want us, crud like that. Maybe we all believed it for a while. I don't know why, when we all knew that Dad was the only one who ever really took care of us. And I was the oldest; I shouldn't have turned against him. I don't even know why I keep on fighting him . . . except that he seems to be right all the time, and I can't stand that. He can be a very annoying person," he said flatly.

"Look, Tom . . ."

"He has a lot of love to give," Tom interrupted her.

"I'm not saying he's not occasionally annoying, but he really does have a lot of love inside him. He can come on sometimes like a ton of bricks, so don't think I don't understand, Susan. Like I'll probably be going to college, maybe even as soon as January; I've got all the credits I need. And Dad may not buy it yet, but what I really want is my own apartment. I'll be eighteen by then, so if he makes you uptight, you can come over and stay with me. Any time you ever want to. You're family, Susan, and I know he can get really annoying on occasion—"

"Tom."

"You're going to have a baby. We know. Lanna called Dad."

Susan closed her eyes, hating Lanna, hating Griff.

"He's got a big thing for babies. He always has." Tom hesitated. "Actually, he seems to have a pretty big thing for you, and like I know he can be really annoying on occasion—"

"Honey, I get the drift," Susan said desperately.

"I thought you would. I knew from the beginning I could talk to you, Susan."

A rap on the door, and there was Barbara.

"I'm nowhere near through," Tom growled.

"Quit sounding like you know it all just because you're older," Barbara snapped. She stepped in, her dark eyes shifting rapidly from place to place, conveying an anxiety that Susan was beginning to recognize all too well. Tom stood up, staring at Susan. In a moment, he was gone, and Barbara had folded herself up in the corduroy chair. She didn't say a single word until Tom had closed the door and she had pleated a fold in her sweat shirt three times.

"Susan, you don't understand," she volunteered finally. "You just don't understand anything."

For the first time in twenty minutes, Susan found that she could breathe effortlessly. Barbara was not likely to wring out her heart and offer up her soul. "I never said

I understood anything, Barbara, and you didn't have to come here to—"

"Mom hates you," Barbara interrupted flatly. "Like I have to stand by her, you know?"

"I know," Susan said quietly.

"Like who else will stick up for her but me? The boys don't count; they're not the same thing at all as mother-daughter . . ."

"I know, honey."

Silence reverberated in the little office. Barbara pleated her sweatshirt a few more times. "I was trying to do my best by Mom, you know?"

"I never doubted that," Susan said gently. "Barbara, it's all right . . ."

"Like I really *didn't* know those boys were coming to that party," Barbara burst out angrily. "For that matter, Mom never let me have a party. She never even let us have friends over. Too much mess, she said. And nobody needs to make my lunch for me, Susan. For godsake, I could make peanut butter and jelly sandwiches when I was five. And I'd hate to have to tell you the times Mom pulled a disappearing act on us, even back when Tiger was really little. If Dad had ever known the kind of meals I put together—"

At Susan's shocked look, Barbara's expression hardened. "Don't you say a word against her," she snapped.

"Have I ever said a word against your mother?"

"No," Barbara admitted, and lowered her eyes. "Sometimes I feel so tied up in knots I can't see straight."

"Oh, honey . . ."

Barbara stood up, stuck her hands in her pockets, and glared at Susan. "*Don't* you leave my father," she said flatly.

"I . . ."

"And it's a stupid way to run a house. Letting Tiger walk all over you with those stupid animals. You think we can't all eat the same stupid thing for breakfast? And like when were you going to get around to saying something about my room? Mom would have had a conniption. *Don't* you leave my father," she said angrily.

"I..."

"I'll baby-sit, you know. Whenever you want, and don't think I don't know anything. I took care of Tiger all the time when he was little. I like little kids. Really. You probably think because I've been so—"

"Barbara..."

But the tape wasn't quite ready to run down. "You'd be surprised, Susan, but I can bring the whole family around when I want to. Dad's not so easy to handle anymore, but the boys...they can fold a few clothes and do a few dishes. You'll see..."

Barbara finally left, closing the door behind her. The shock of sudden silence hit Susan like a bomb. She sat totally still behind the desk, afraid to move for fear Griff would conjure up more children out of thin air and send them in to splinter her heart in another thousand pieces. How *could* he? How *could* he have involved them? And as for Lanna broadcasting that she was pregnant...

She rubbed her fingers against her temples, trying desperately not to admit how much the children had gotten to her. So she loved the urchins; she already knew that. Tiger, who liked to discuss his entire life in detail before breakfast, and Tom, who was determined to grow up too fast and drive his father up the wall. Even Barbara, perhaps especially Barbara, so desperately belligerent as an act of loyalty to her mother, her big eyes so terribly vulnerable...

"Susan?"

Her head jerked up at the sound of Lanna's voice from behind the closed door; one hand brushed rapidly at her eyes. "I'll be out in a minute."

"You don't need to," Lanna called smoothly. "It's nearly twelve, though, and I've gotten rid of the crowd. I just wanted to tell you that the CLOSED sign is going up."

"Fine."

"I'll be upstairs if you need anything."

"No," Susan said quietly. "Everything's fine."

She stared at the closed door until she heard the sound of Lanna's footsteps fading; then she got up from behind the desk. *Why* couldn't she get her head together? She had been so very sure they were doing the right thing when they got married, and she'd known all about his children then. She'd known in her heart that the marriage would work. It had seemed so simple. All it took was enough love; she knew she had enough love, and she knew Griff had enough love . . .

She opened the door of her office. A silent shop greeted her, late fall sunlight glinting in faded yellow patches through the two windows. She let down the blinds, removed the key from beneath the register, and remembered distractedly that she'd walked here. She didn't have a car; she didn't have a change of clothes; Lanna's sweater was too tight; she was hungry and miserable and didn't have the least idea where she was going.

But she went. At least as far as opening the door, closing it, and fitting in the key into the lock.

"Susan?"

She whirled at the sound of Griff's voice, her face turning pale. The Viking's features were carved in granite, his eyes boring into hers like some piercing stab of life.

"I . . ." She took the key out of the lock and put it in her pocket, not looking at him. "I didn't mean to just . . . leave. I wasn't *leaving* you, Griff. I can't even imagine . . . *really* leaving. I just needed a little time alone. If you'll just give me a little time . . ."

"No way," Griff said quietly. His voice came out in a growl. "You're coming with me."

15

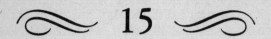

THE VISE THAT enclosed Susan's hand would have put a handcuff to shame. Griff had left his car in the no-parking zone directly in front of the shop. Before she realized what was happening, her head seemed to be leaning back against the soft upholstery of the passenger seat. She was locked in; Griff had bolted around to his side and was starting the engine.

"That was unforgivable. Sending the children," she accused him uncertainly.

"Tough."

The conversation wasn't moving any too smoothly. "You don't have to sound quite so angry . . ."

"Madder than hell," he corrected.

"With me."

"With you," he agreed.

"Griff," she said quietly, "you're not the only one capable of having an honest temper tantrum on occasion. I wouldn't push it, if I were you."

The words had come from nowhere and were so out of character that Griff shot her a startled look. "I think, Susan," he said gently, "that that's exactly what we're going to have to do. Push it."

"I . . ."

The conversation wasn't just difficult; it was impossible. Susan subsided, staring out at the Saturday drivers, weaving in and out of traffic, determined to have their weekend fun as dangerously as possible. Speed was the essence; murder the sideline. They arrived safe and sound, but the place they arrived at took Susan back.

ANDERSON'S, the sign said. The plant was a long, low mass of glass and concrete, nestled back from the road among trees and shrubs. Griff parked the car near the entrance, came around to her side, opened the door, and waited patiently.

She just looked at him as she unfolded her legs and got out of the car.

"The kids are at my sister's, but this is the one place where I know no one will interrupt us."

On a Saturday, that was undoubtedly true, but she was suspicious of his motives. First he'd sent the children to soften her up, and now he expected her to do battle on his turf. She hadn't known when she married him that he fought dirty. There was no one but a watchman to let them in. The corridors were yawning empty; the lights were dimmed; the switchboard silent; the elevator creaked plaintively... They got off on the third floor; Susan knew the route to his office.

She led the way, her back rigid, not looking at Griff. Her heart felt sick; she didn't really know what to say to him. He opened the door, and she walked into his private working domain; she heard the click of the door as it locked behind her like some frightening omen.

Executive elegance was not the style of this room. Griff was a working man; there was a brown leather couch, yes, but only for those occasions when he catnapped while working extra long hours. The gold carpet was deep-piled only for the purpose of blocking out the sounds of machinery, and Griff's walnut desk was piled high with paperwork. The credenza beyond held a pair of phones, a computer terminal, and a small, square refrigerator where he stocked supplies for five-minute lunches of the kind she herself usually ate. He strode past her and crouched down in front of it now, a thousand times more calm than she was. "Have you had lunch?"

"No. Griff, I couldn't be less hungry." Was he insane? The last thing on either of their minds was food.

"You didn't eat much at breakfast, I'm guessing..." Griff started piling food on top of his desk. "A cheese sandwich?"

Her stomach turned a somersault. "God, no!"

Still on his haunches, he swiveled around to look at her. All that lethal fire in his eyes was suddenly tempered by a sudden quirk of a smile. "So your problem is going to be cheese, is it?"

"Griff..."

"Sit down, Susan. We're going to have a hell of a fight. We might as well eat first."

He might have been saying that tonight there would be a 10 percent chance of rain; his tone of voice was that conversational. She slumped down on the couch, bewildered, exhausted, and increasingly angry. He handed her a small carton of milk, then two slabs of French bread with peanut butter in the middle, then an apple. He took a slice of cheese for himself and sat back behind his desk, calmly watching her eat.

She really didn't intend to eat a bite. She had a terror of being sick to her stomach and dizzy again, and yet eating bought her a measure of time. His children were small guns, but they'd been effective enough. She wasn't ready for the barrage he was about to hit her with. She wanted just what she had asked him for. Time. Privacy. Just because she was a wife and stepmother didn't mean she didn't have a right to those things.

She wiped her hands on a napkin, settled back in a corner of the leather couch, and stared at him. "Griff, have I done anything so terrible?" she demanded finally, since he refused to break his silence. "Everyone has to have a little time to herself—"

"Occasionally, yes, and you need more privacy than most people do. But not today, Susan. If I let you spend a few more hours alone today, you'll worry yourself inside out. You'll wall all your doubts up inside you, and I'll never hear a word about what's troubling you. Now, *talk,* Susan; let's hear it."

She shook her head. "Taking off in the middle of the night was stupid; you don't have to tell me that. I didn't mean to cause such a rumpus. I just couldn't sleep."

"Be honest, Susan," he demanded. "What's troubling you, really?"

She glared at him. "I want to be *alone!*"

"Take one step toward that door and see what happens," he suggested, but his voice was curiously gentle.

Which didn't make sense. "Griff. I can't explain . . ."

"*Try,* honey."

The gentleness in his voice threatened to produce tears in her eyes, but she fought them with her anger. She leaped to her feet. "Look. I never have any time alone with you. I *need* time with you. I love you, and I need to just be with you. Alone. Suddenly, we can only make love when the lights are out and we're both too tired. Suddenly, when I've got a thousand things to tell you, I have to save them all up for the minute and a half when I can catch you, and I end up never saying them at all. You think I don't love the children, Griff? Well, you're dead wrong. But I want more than just to be a mother for your kids!"

Griff was around the desk before she could finish, his shoulders rippling and a fiery gleam in his eyes. "Why didn't you tell me they were giving you trouble? Why couldn't you come to me about Barbara's party? They were creating a little hell for you, and you didn't trust me enough to tell me about it! They were damned happy being waited on hand and foot. Tiger's under the impression you want a houseful of animals, and Tom thinks you *love* rock music turned up full blast. *Why* didn't you tell me what the devil was going on?"

"*Nothing* was going on!"

"You thought I expected you to put up with their nonsense," he growled. "That's what kills me, Susan."

She hesitated, unable to bear his fury any longer. She

looked down at the carpet with miserable, doe-soft eyes, her heart still beating like a tom-tom. "You could have seen—"

"I *would* have seen," he corrected. "In very short order. I didn't plan on having all three kids descend on us at the same time I had two weeks of crisis here at work—but long before that, you were having trouble with the children, Susan, and you never said one word. You were all smiles whenever I asked you—"

"You asked me about Barbara," she cut him off defensively. "But I couldn't break trust with her by running to you like a tattletale, Griff. I was having a hard enough time—"

"So I'm just beginning to understand—but this has nothing to do with Barbara. Or the other two children. It has to do with trust, between you and me—and you should have come to me. The kids adore you, Susan, but I knew that would happen before they even laid eyes on you. Sure, that mattered to me, but if you think I married you to provide a mother for the kids, you're out of your mind. I married you solely because I love you so much it hurts, and in the relationship I thought we had, it's understood that we turn to each other when one of us gets into deep water."

Lord, he exhausted her. Everything seemed so simple when he said it. Nothing had been that simple when it was happening. The kids *did* care; they *were* on her side; they'd told her so very clearly this morning, but it had not seemed so obvious living with them day by day. And that Griff was willing to back her up when she felt herself floundering had seemed even less obvious.

"Griff," she started unhappily, and stopped. She sighed. "I hear you. And I think it's past time I confessed I did fall into deep water, and that frightens the devil out of me..."

He slowly exhaled the last of his anger in one long breath. He was there suddenly, cradling her to himself, sinking into the leather couch with her on his lap. "And you damn well better believe we can get you out of it.

Together," he whispered. His hand stroked her hair, urging her cheek to his shoulder. "The kids have obviously been working very hard to show you their worst side. And we've had trial after trial thrown at us in these first months when what we both wanted most was just to be alone together, and that wasn't fair, love. Some of the problems will be very easy to solve. We'll hire extra help for you, both at work and at home. The kids—all I had to do was point out to them that they had made you unhappy. I know you'll see some drastic changes in their attitudes. The house is all but done, and I can delegate a great deal of work here at the office to allow me to be home more..."

She looked up at him. "Such a tough group you all are," she murmured wryly. "Just like that book. The four of you getting so very tough with me this morning...showing your love. I do believe the principle is finally managing to sink in—but it was hard, Griff. I wanted to be perfect for you; I didn't want you to know I was having trouble handling anything. I was so unhappy at the thought of disappointing you."

"That was never possible." His lips softly rubbed a message on her forehead, her nose, her cheeks. "The kids need a lot of attention right now, Susan, but giving love also means setting limits—for them and for us. I *need* time with you. I *need* privacy with you... and I'm going to get those things, just as you have the right to stand up for what you want and need. Life's far too short, love, and I had to live far too many years without you. I'm not saying there won't be upheavals from time to time. There will, of course, but I promise that, no matter what happens, I won't lose sight of you and your needs, Susan. I love you far, far too much..."

He wasn't alone in those feelings. Susan sighed, relaxing. She knew he would keep his promises, because he was that kind of man, but it was more than that. It was that he understood; that he wanted and needed the same things she did. She curled her body to fit the contours of his, winding her arms around his neck as his mouth settled on hers, slow and hard.

"You want the baby?" she whispered against him.

"You mean the one with the big gray eyes and silky dark hair who's going to throw us all into chaos again in a few months?"

Susan smiled, closing her eyes. "I think," she said absently, "that must be the one."

"I think," Griff said just as absently, "that there isn't anything I could possibly want more than I want your baby."

Her fingertips slowly traced the line of his jaw. "You only *think* so?"

"I know so. And don't start worrying, Susan. Keep in mind that we have a few live-in baby-sitters, that I can whip up a mean lasagne, and that once upon a time I could change a diaper faster than the speed of sound. Furthermore, I'm an expert on colic. Did you know that?"

"I never did," she said gravely.

"Just maybe there are a few other things you don't know." He shifted her again, and she suddenly found herself lying flat on the cushions staring up into Griff's eyes. Devil eyes. There was a slash of a smile on his lips. "For one thing, pregnant fathers need a lot of rest."

"Pregnant . . ." She chuckled. *Rest* was the last thing his eyes were suggesting. "Griff," she whispered, "you know darn well this couch is too narrow."

"We'll manage."

They did.

WONDERFUL ROMANCE NEWS!

Do you know about the exciting SECOND CHANCE AT LOVE/TO HAVE AND TO HOLD newsletter? Are you on our *free* mailing list? If reading all about your favorite authors, getting sneak previews of their latest releases, and being filled in on all the latest happenings and events in the romance world sounds good to you, then you'll love our SECOND CHANCE AT LOVE and TO HAVE AND TO HOLD Romance News.

If you'd like to be added to our mailing list, just fill out the coupon below and send it in...and we'll send you your *free* newsletter every three months—hot off the press.

☐ ***Yes, I would like to receive your free SECOND CHANCE AT LOVE/TO HAVE AND TO HOLD newsletter.***

Name ______________________________

Address ____________________________

City ______________ **State/Zip** __________

Please return this coupon to:

Berkley Publishing
200 Madison Avenue, New York, New York 10016
Att: Irene Majuk